WHOSE KNIFE IS IT ANYWAY?

OTHER NOVELS in the Grandmothers, Incorporated book series by Evans and Rhodes

Grandmothers, Incorporated

When a former high school classmate dies, three "sixty-something" widows are determined to prove the cause was foul play, even if they have to turn the lives of everyone around them upside down in their hilarious quest.

Saving Sin City

Take two fun loving grandmothers and one religious zealot, put them in Las Vegas and Sin City will never be the same again. It's fun in the sun for the amateur sleuths from Grandmothers, Incorporated as they go on a holiday that won't easily be forgotten.

There's Something Wrong with Miss Zelda

On vacation, the amateur sleuths of Grandmothers, Incorporated discover that their friend Miss Zelda has some major skeletons falling out of her closet. Mystery, intrigue and laughs abound in this third installment of the Grandmothers, Incorporated book series.

From the Stage to the Page

Two hilarious stage plays featuring characters from the Grandmothers, Incorporated cozy book series.

All books are available in Ebook and Paperback format on Amazon.com and Ebook format on Smashwords.com.

WHOSE KNIFE IS IT ANYWAY?

A novel by

L. Barnett Evans
And
C.V. Rhodes

GRINCO, L.L.C.
Indianapolis, Indiana

WHOSE KNIFE IS IT ANYWAY?
Published by GRINCO, LLC
P.O. Box 781142
Indianapolis, Indiana 46278

First Edition

ISBN: 978-0-9838614-8-5

DEDICATION

This book is dedicated to all grandmothers who stand in the gap for their families, offering a foundation of strength, courage, love and moral fortitude.

ACKNOWLEDGMENTS

Thank you to the members of the Sisters-in-Crime Mystery Writers' critique group that worked so diligently on providing feedback in the development of this book. Your suggestions made the work better than we could have imagined.

To Judy Bullard of Custom Ebook Covers, thank you for the creative covers you have designed for our books, *Saving Sin City*, *There's Something Wrong with Miss Zelda?*, *From the Page to the Stage,* and *Whose Knife is it Anyway?* What would we have done without you?

CHAPTER 1

"You did what?" Bryant Bell bellowed.

Beatrice Bell didn't let the incredulous look on her son's face impede her pride in her accomplishment. Proudly, she repeated her announcement.

"I got my P. I. license."

"But you're in your sixties!" Bryant croaked.

"That's right, and I am now certified by the state of Indiana as a Private Investigator."

"You're kidding." Bea's best friend, Hattie Collier, looked as dumbfounded as Bea's son.

Her other best friend, Connie Palmer, laughed out loud. "What other jokes do you have for us, Bea?"

"Oh, it's a joke." The relief in Joshua Pierce's voice was palpable. "Thank goodness!"

Bea glowered at her handsome boyfriend. With his silver mane, athletic build and great disposition, there were times this man made her feel absolutely giddy. This wasn't one of those times.

"No, it is *not* a joke," she told him coolly.

Bea had been beside herself with excitement when she called her family and friends to invite them to her house for dinner. She told each of them that she had something important to announce. All through dinner they had bombarded her with questions about her mysterious announcement. Now that it had been made, it was being treated as a joke. That didn't sit well with her.

The only one who seemed to be taking her seriously was Tina, the granddaughter that she shared with Connie.

The girl was staying with Bea while her mother was out of town on business.

"I believe you, Grandmother," the fifteen year old declared. She flashed a smile so like her deceased father's that for a moment Bea lost focus. Her oldest son, James, Jr. had been married to Connie's daughter, Ernestine. He had died from cancer years ago and his only child was the center of Bea's life.

"Thank you, baby." She kissed the girl softly. "At least somebody takes me seriously." She glared at the others. "As for all of you doubters—" Picking up an envelope off a table, she removed its contents, then held up her certificate for all to see. "Here's the proof." She thrust it toward her son.

Plucking it from her hand, he scanned it briefly.

"What in the hell is the Get Your Man Institute for Private Eyes? Where's that located?"

"On the internet, and don't you dare use that kind of language with me."

"On the internet!" Bryant exploded. "You mean to tell me that you got your detective license on-line?"

"Yes," Bea replied defiantly, determined not to let his reaction dampen her spirits.

She loved her son dearly. He was a wonderful man, and good looking too. Like his late father, his complexion was a warm, chestnut brown and his eyes were dark and expressive, but he was in his forties and ought to be out looking for a wife instead of meddling in her business.

"How much did all of this cost?' Hattie inquired.

"The license fee was $150.00."

"Is that all?" Connie's interest was piqued.

"Yeah, girl, and all I had to do was fill out an application."

Bryant was not impressed. "Let me get this straight. I went to college, majored in Criminal Justice..."

"But I wanted you to be an engineer," Bea reminded him. He ignored her.

"I went through rigorous training at the police academy to become a member of the Indianapolis Police Department..."

"And I'm proud of you, sweetheart."

"Then, after years of paying my dues, I finally get promoted and became an investigator, when I could have saved myself a lot of time and trouble by simply going on line."

Bea shrugged. "Who knew?"

"What did you have to do to qualify for this certificate?" Josh carefully scrutinized the official looking document Bryant handed him.

"Well I had to be at least 21 years old and have no felony convictions. On top of that, I had to demonstrate the skills and knowledge on how to operate a firm and do investigations."

"And you have experience doing this?" Josh raised a skeptical brow.

Hattie piped in. "I don't know if Bea told you, but the three of us have solved several crimes. There was the Frank Schaffer case..."

"And the bust at the drug house," Connie added.

"Don't forget the incident with Miss Zelda," Bea reminded them.

"And of course all of you must remember how *I* solved the mystery in Las Vegas practically by myself," Hattie bragged.

Bea shot her an exasperated look. "This is not about you." She turned to Josh. "And to finish answering your question, I also had to have an Indiana business license to get certified."

"You've got a business license?" Hattie looked surprised.

"Yes I do, from the State of Indiana. It didn't cost that much."

Bryant threw his arms in the air in frustration. "Oh, great! Since when did you become a business woman? You're a retired city administrator, Mom! *Retired! Remember?* "

Bea tried to remain patient. "Not any more dear. Connie owns and runs Palmer Realty. Hattie started, her funeral consultant business, Half Way Home, and now I'm the proud owner of Grandmothers, Incorporated."

"Grandmothers, Incorporated!" Hattie and Connie screeched in delight.

"Private Investigators!" Bea took her certificate from Josh and held it high in the air. "Ladies and gentlemen, Grandmothers, Incorporated, is officially in business!"

The three women squealed with excitement, hugging and laughing exuberantly as they gave each other high fives.

"You did it, Bea!"

"Congratulations!"

"Way to go, Grandmother!" Tina joined the trio, giving Bea a big hug. "I've got to spread the word!" She started tweeting on her cell phone.

Josh looked on in silent disapproval. Bryant made an attempt to remain calm. It didn't work.

"Listen, Mom, while I applaud your initiative, let me remind you that I am a decorated member of IPD and I cannot have my mother running around Indianapolis playing detective. It's dangerous, and those streets are no place for a bunch of old ladies playing games."

As soon as the words left his mouth Bryant realized his mistake. Josh groaned in anticipation of the eruption. It didn't take long.

"What?" Bea demanded. The look she gave Bryant was primal.

"Who in the hell are you calling *old*?" Connie yelled.

Hattie held her hands skyward, "Lord! Don't let me have to hurt Bea's child."

Bryant had opened a can of worms. The barrage of barbs and insults came fast and furious. Hands were placed on hips, heads were rolling, fingers were wagging in his face. Tina recorded the action on her cell phone. Wisely, Josh stayed out of the fray. Bryant was on his own.

He accepted the consequences of having misspoken until enough was enough. Placing his fingers between his lips he released a piercing whistle.

"Okay! Cool it!"

The shrill sound and commanding order brought gradual compliance. Three pairs of defiant eyes threw daggers his way. Bryant was humbled.

"Okay, I'm sorry. Believe me, I know that you three are far from being helpless old ladies."

"You better believe it," spat Bea.

"And, Mom, please don't remind me of how you and your friends helped get me my promotion with that raid on the drug house."

"And don't you forget it." Miss Hattie couldn't resist one final jab.

"The three of you are beautiful, intelligent and more than capable of doing great things, but Mother, surely you must understand that getting a piece of paper over the internet doesn't mean that you're a real Private Investigator. Come on, now!"

Bea disagreed. "The state of Indiana seems to think so."

"And they trump you any day," Connie declared.

"Amen!" Hattie seconded.

Bryant thought it best to retreat. "I tell you what, Mom. I'm going home. I've got an early day tomorrow, and don't you have to pack for that woman's retreat the three of you are attending? "

Bea stood arms tightly folded. She didn't feel very forgiving. *Old ladies indeed!* "That's right."

Bryant started backing toward the front door. "How many days are you going to be in those woods?"

"We leave on Thursday and we'll be back on Sunday," Hattie answered for Bea.

"Good, that will give both of us time to clear our heads about this P.I. thing." Bryant took Tina's phone out of her hand as he was retreating.

"Hey, Uncle Bryant!"

"No Facebook." Her uncle deleted the video before handing the cell phone back to her. "Find something else to post."

"Awww, man." The look she gave her uncle now resembled those of the other females in the room.

"I don't need a conference to clear my head," snapped Bea. "My mind is clear as a bell. And I plan on engaging in quiet contemplation and spiritual growth while I'm gone."

"How's that supposed to happen?" Connie scoffed. "You told me that we're going to be stuck in the woods with the worst bunch of two faced, backstabbing, blabber mouths in Indianapolis."

Josh looked confused. "But Bea, you said the ladies volunteered for this retreat to mend hard feelings between some churches."

"That's right," Bea assured him.

Connie rubbed her hands together eagerly. "And I can't wait to see how this turns out. "

"Connie, you're just going to start some devilment," Hattie chastised

"Sounds interesting." Bryant had reached the front door and couldn't wait to exit. "Well, have a good time all of you. And Mom, I'll give you a call before you go on that trip with the Road Warriors..."

"The Road Wanderers."

"I stand corrected. Who knows, maybe you ladies will have a story to tell when you come back from your trip. Love you, Mom. Good night all."

"Love you too." How could she help but love him. He was her baby, despite his big mouth.

Bryant hurried out the door. Bea turned to Josh, the remaining dissenter in the room. "Have you got anything else to say?"

Josh swallowed hard. His mama didn't raise a fool.

"Just let me know what time the three of you are leaving on Thursday and I'll pick you up."

CHAPTER 2

Several clusters of women stood in the parking lot of stately Mt. Malachi Baptist church laughing, chatting and enjoying shared camaraderie. Conversation gradually ceased when Joshua Pierce's Aston Martin pulled into the lot and rolled to a stop. It was followed by Connie's small sedan which parked behind him.

Necks craned to see the driver of the luxury vehicle, and when he stepped out there were murmurs of admiration. When Bea emerged from the passenger side there was a collective gasp.

Hattie and Connie got out of her car and went to the trunk to remove their luggage. Connie then walked over to where Bea stood behind Josh's car waiting for him to remove her bag.

"Oh, oh, Bea," she teased. "Looks like you gave the gossipers something to talk about on the trip. I told you to show Josh off a long time ago."

"I couldn't care less," Bea huffed. "Let them talk. As long as these hussies keep their hands off the merchandise..."

Hattie cut her short. "Listen you two! This trip was organized to heal bad feelings, so let's change your attitudes right now." With luggage in hand, she stalked off to find Dorothy and Thelma.

"I guess she told us," Connie scoffed.

"Oh be quiet," Bea grunted. "You know doggone well you're just going on this trip to meddle. You don't even go to church."

"I do, sometimes. But I have to admit that I do plan on sitting back these next few days and enjoying the fireworks."

When Hattie reached Dorothy Riggs and Thelma Reeves she could tell that the two friends were upset. It was through their travel club that she had helped plan this trip and they wasted no time complaining to her.

"We've got trouble," an exasperated Dorothy began. "Me and Thelma thought we'd have everyone sit next to a member of another church—you know, mix it up so people could get acquainted."

"But the way these women are acting, you would think we asked them to drink poison." Thelma gave a disgusted grunt.

Dorothy shook her head in agreement. "Lord, that's the truth. You might call this trip a Reconciliation Retreat, but so far the spirit of cooperation ain't working."

Hattie frowned. "Don't worry, I'll take care of that later. Right now we'd better get the meeting started."

The three women moved to the front of the gathering.

"Ladies!" Dorothy tried to get their attention. The chatter continued.

Thelma tried, with an increase in volume. "Ladies!" She was also ignored.

Hattie marched over to Josh, who had stayed to see Bea off.

"Josh, could you help us get everyone's attention?"

Many of the women were throwing admiring glances his way, leaving Josh both confused and amused by the assembly. Doing as Hattie requested, he put his fingers between his lips and let out a piercing whistle. The incessant chattering was replaced by indignation.

"What in the world?"

"Has he lost his mind?"

With a nod of thanks to Josh for focusing attention in her direction, Hattie announced, "Okay, Christian women, it's time to meet in the church dining hall before the bus arrives."

"Follow us," Dorothy directed. With varied degrees of compliance, the ladies did as told.

****

When everyone had settled in their seats inside the church, Dorothy and Thelma stood in front of the contingent. Some of the women were receptive, others appeared indifferent.

"Ladies, as most of you might know Thelma and I started Road Wanderers years ago to travel with some friends in order to have fun."

"It seemed that many of you who had retired wanted to do more than park your carcasses in a chair, play bingo, do crossword puzzles or watch soap operas," said Thelma, "and traveling to new places was the perfect solution."

"With Thelma's skills at getting cheap group rates for hotels and entertainment venues, our trips have been very successful," Dorothy boasted.

"And hopefully, the trip we're going to take today will be the best one of all." Thelma broke into a bright smile. "You, the members from the Church of the Living Unity of Christ's Kingdom Missionary Baptist church or CLUCK Baptist as it is so fondly called."

"I ain't never been fond of it being called that," someone in the back of the room shouted.

Thelma continued undaunted. "Twelve Disciples Christian church and Mt. Malachi Baptist have all signed up for this church retreat..."

"And we all have to thank our friend, Hattie Collier of Mt. Malachi, for this splendid idea," Dorothy interjected. "Hattie, come join us."

Thelma and Dorothy led the applause, joined by an enthusiastic ovation from Hattie's friends and fellow church members as she came forward. There was polite acknowledgement from the others in attendance.

A grinning Hattie was more than glad to be recognized for her Christian contributions. "Thank you everyone, and in the spirit of the Lord and of this gathering, I know that you'll cooperate with our trip coordinators and sit on the bus according to the seats they have..."

"Hold it, Hattie!" Once again the cry came from the back of the room.

Lucretia Martin, the seventy-something year old widow of Mt. Malachi's former pastor, made her way to the front where Hattie, Dorothy and Thelma stood. Because the current pastor, Reverend Samuel Trees was a widower, the formidable Lucretia believed the title of first lady automatically reverted to her by default. It certainly did not belong to Hattie Collier, the woman that the present pastor was courting. Lucretia made sure to stand directly in front of Hattie.

"I'll handle this," she told the trio. "As you know, a first lady, has experience organizing." She addressed the gathering. "Ladies, if we can each sit next to someone you don't know or who goes to a church other than your own, it would facilitate what I feel we want to accomplish."

Bea was standing with Josh at the back of the room, but she made certain that her comment could be heard. "We? We who, Lucretia? You didn't have a thing to do with organizing this retreat. Hattie did."

A member of Mt. Malachi took offense at how her former first lady was being addressed. "Mother Lucretia is an elder in our church. Have some respect."

A CLUCK Baptist member came to Bea's defense. "But she's right. You would think that you'd give credit where credit is due."

A Twelve Disciples church member spoke up. "Anyway, Miss Lucretia's husband is dead. Why does she think she's a first lady? Reverend Trees has been the pastor at your church for years. What's she first lady of?"

Eyes widened and backs stiffened as malevolent glares passed between the members of the three churches represented. Rumblings of dissent began to rise. Chuckling, Josh teased Bea.

"Look what you started."

"Oh be quiet." She rolled her eyes at him.

"Ladies! Ladies! Raising her hands to gain their attention, Thelma tried to halt the rising rebellion, but the gauntlet had been thrown.

LaVerne Nelson, another member of CLUCK Baptist spoke up. "All I've got to say is that if what Bea said was disrespectful, some people must not know what respect means!"

"When did CLUCK Baptist become familiar with respect?" Pearl Mason shot back.

Hattie's eyes slid to Dorothy and then to Thelma. The two women looked shell shocked. World War III was surely looming. Every woman in the room was aware of the feud between Pearl Mason, the pastor's wife at Twelve Disciples Christian, and LaVerne Nelson.

When CLUCK Baptist sponsored its big "all city" church musical a couple of years ago, Laverne had been the president of the planning committee. She and Pearl had been on speaking terms then and Laverne's committee had picked Pearl's brain about how to pull it off and who to invite. It was well known that Reverend Mason's wife had a great deal of influence in the city's religious community. She could be quite charming as well as politically savvy.

Pearl also fancied herself as being a great gospel singer. Although she was in her sixties, she had dreams of launching a recording career. In exchange for her ideas and contacts Pearl was to be listed as a soloist in the program. Yet, when the program came out, not only was she not on it, but her church wasn't invited to the event. The memory of that insult and betrayal was still fresh. Lavern and Pearl hadn't spoken since—that is, until now.

"Lord have mercy! These women are too old to be acting like fools!" Hattie croaked. "We have to do something!" It wasn't farfetched to think that this confrontation might end up in a fist fight.

It was the petty feuds, slights and exchange of insults that had amassed over the years between members of the three churches represented in the room that resulted in the Reconciliation Retreat. Each of the churches was highly respected in the Indianapolis community, but the growing animosities between their members threatened to erode any influence the institutions might have, especially among young people where it was sorely needed. Something *had* to be done.

At this particular moment, Hattie knew just what to do. Throwing her arms skyward, she called on a greater force.

"Heavenly Father, this is a day that you have made, so please help these people to be glad and rejoice in it."

As the women began to realize that Hattie Collier was praying they slowly transferred their attention to her. She was known to take prayer to a whole new level. Dorothy's cell phone rang and she stepped aside to take the call, as Hattie continued to plead her case to a Higher Power.

"Lord, we ask you to forgive these women for their uncooperative spirit. Teach them to fear you, for your wrath is mighty! Sweet Jesus, I want to see love and harmony on this trip so that none of us here will find ourselves at the fiery gates of hell for not cooperating. In your precious name, Amen."

"Amen," a few scattered voices echoed.

Dorothy stepped back into the room and addressed the women. "I just heard from the bus driver. He's a block away. Now he's not our usual driver, but I heard he was good. So, come on ladies, grab your bags and let's go outside."

Tension was still high as Pearl and Laverne glared at each other, but like the others they did as asked and started filing out of the room. Thelma gave a sigh of relief and whispered to Hattie, "It looks like we avoided that disaster."

"Thank God. Let's hope that things get better rather than worse."

The words were barely out of Hattie's mouth when their charter bus came barreling down the street toward the church. The big vehicle tilted as the driver made a sharp turn into the parking lot, coming to an abrupt stop with tires squealing. Several women screamed and ran for their lives.

"What the hell?" Connie was dumbfounded. "I thought Dorothy said he was a good driver!"

Alarmed, Josh pulled Bea back to safety. "If this guy drives this foolishly, I don't know if I want you going on this trip."

"That makes two of us," Bea agreed.

Dorothy and Thelma approached the bus cautiously just as the doors flung open. They gawked at the dark-skinned man who stared back at them. Leaning on the steering wheel, the driver gave them a lopsided grin.

"Ladies, your chariot awaits."

"I don't think so!" a member of the group shouted defiantly.

"You're not scattering our bodies all over the highway!" another one proclaimed.

"We're not getting on that bus with *him*!" That declaration became the consensus. It looked as though the trip might be over before it began.

Hattie, Dorothy and Thelma coaxed, pleaded and finally compromised to get everyone aboard. If the women would get on the bus, they could sit where they wanted.

"I'm not going to be bothered with a bunch of nagging females," the bus driver stated arrogantly.

"Excuse me." Dorothy glared at him. "Maybe I need to call your boss for a new driver."

"That's exactly what we should do," Hattie agreed.

Unnerved, the driver stared at them. After thinking about it for a moment, he tried to look as contrite as possible.

"I'm sorry I ruffled your feathers, ladies. How about we get this show on the road?"

"That's not much of an apology. I suggest you watch your step from now on and drive like you got good sense." Dorothy gave him a look that said she meant business.

Still grumbling, the women clambered aboard, delighted to ignore the seating plan.

"Ladies, I need your attention." Thelma clapped her hands loudly. "Quiet please, so we can do the roll call." She was ignored.

Tired of Thelma's polite request, Dorothy stood up and barked, "Shut up so we can hear!"

There was instant silence—for about 15 seconds..

"Dorothy you're not talking to a bunch of children."

"She must be having flashbacks about driving that school bus."

"She's not going to talk to me like that."

After waving goodbye to a departing Josh, Bea came to a half standing position- to seek out the source of the complaints. As she studied her fellow passengers she frowned, then leaned over to Hattie. "Where's Miss Fanny? Where's your mother-in-law?"

Hattie shrugged. "I don't know. She said that she was coming."

A half block away, the continuous blare of a car horn could be heard. The noise came closer and closer, until a red Mercedes screeched into the parking lot and pulled beside the bus. Miss Fanny was behind the wheel.

Hattie muttered a prayer, asking for the strength to endure her mother-in-law through this weekend. She had hoped that the crabby octogenarian wouldn't show up.

With her luggage in tow, Miss Fanny climbed aboard the bus and announced to no one in particular. "Whew! I made it! And in one piece too. Not bad for a woman in her eighties, huh?" Glancing at the man behind the wheel, she realized that he wasn't the Road Wanderers' usual bus driver. "Who are you?"

"I'm George Hadley, the substitute driver."

"Oh, that's why I had to struggle with my bag. Our regular driver, Mr. Sweeney, is a gentleman."

"Well, Sweeney ain't here."

Looking him up and down, Miss Fanny griped, "Young man, I don't think we're going to get along." Taking a seat, she barked, "You can go now."

CHAPTER 3

Dorothy had never seen such a disgruntled looking group in her life. Grabbing the microphone to the bus PA system, she called out. "Are you ladies ready for a movie?" The response was weak. She held out her hand to Thelma for the video but came up empty. She turned to see her partner groping around under her seat.

"Give me the DVD, Thelma."

"I don't see the bag with the movies in it."

"I set it right there under the... Shit!" Dorothy muttered under her breath. "I laid the bag by my chair back in the church dining room!" she confessed aloud.

When she announced a movie wouldn't be forthcoming, an angry rumble emanated throughout the bus.

Dorothy Riggs had been a school bus driver for 25 years and had endured the fighting, screaming and crying of countless numbers of unruly children. Order was something she had always insisted on and order is what she got. Yet, with all of her experience dealing with rowdy children, she had never encountered a group as stubborn as this load of spiteful hens. Exhausted from her efforts to get the slightest bit of cooperation from them, she flopped down in her seat next to Hattie, just behind the bus driver.

"This was your idea, Hattie Collier. We're only twenty minutes into this trip and it's looking like a bust."

"Then you must be doing something wrong," Hattie retorted.

Thelma leaned over her seat behind the pair. "I agree with Dorothy. If we hadn't let you hijack our trip we could be having fun by now. Reconciliation, my foot! Do dogs get along with cats? Do elephants love mice?"

"We're not dogs or cats," Hattie fumed. "We're children of God. We were made a little lower than the angels and we *will* do the right thing."

Loud voices from the back of the bus interrupted their squabble.

"Looks like a couple of those low-down angels are at it" George Hadley cracked. "I can't have all of this noise while I'm driving. Would one of you ladies see to it?"

Hauling herself out of her seat, Hattie marched to the back of the bus. Bea followed her.

"You might need professional backup," she whispered, patting the pants pocket where she had carefully stored a copy of her Private Investigator license. She couldn't wait until she got her PI badge.

When they reached the back, they found Angela Rivers, a member of Twelve Disciples and Lucretia Martin who belonged to Mt. Malachi, leaning into the bus aisle trading barbs. Angela was in her thirties and one of the younger women on the bus.

"Is there a problem back here?" Hattie demanded.

Lucretia pointed at Angela. "There won't be one if missy here learns to respect her elders."

"I'm a grown woman," Angela huffed. "I don't need your permission to speak. Now take your finger out of my face!"

"You're both grown," said Hattie, disgusted by the juvenile behavior. "So, what's going on?"

"I'm tired of hearing her gripe about how she should be sitting toward the front since she's the first lady of Mt. Malachi." Angela gestured toward Lucretia.

Hattie spoke quietly. "Miss Lucretia, our church doesn't have a first lady. You know Reverend Trees is a widower. "

Angela nodded. "And she's not married to Reverend Trees. So how is she a first lady?"

Overhearing Angela's last comment, Miss Fanny hollered from her seat in the front, "You ain't said nothing but the truth." As intended, Lucretia heard her.

"You need to keep your nose out of this Fanny Collier!" she yelled back. "Everybody knows that your daughter-in-law is applying for the job of second wife."

Hattie was speechless but Miss Fanny wasn't. Rising from her seat, she gave the woman a deadly look. "I don't like your tone, Lucretia. Hattie is a widow and the Reverend is a widower. Neither one of them is married and they ain't dead. That means as long as they handle their courtship in a respectable way, you don't have a thing to say."

"And neither does anybody else on this bus," Bea warned, giving those within sight the evil eye. Nobody talked about her friends but her!

Lucretia drew up in indignation, but the demeanor of Bea and Miss Fanny warned her that a reply was better left unsaid.

With that bit of tension having been defused, the bus returned to its original state with the ladies quietly complaining to each other about everything. Another twenty minutes passed and Connie called out from her seat.

"Hey, Dorothy! I forgot I brought a video. Look in my brown bag in the overhead compartment."

"What movie is it?" someone called out.

"Denzel's latest," Connie shouted back. Excited mummers drifted through the bus as the women settled back in anticipation.

Dorothy popped the DVD in the player. The movie queued up. Dramatic music soared throughout the bus' interior as the opening credits began to roll. Denzel's face appeared on the screen. He gave a sexy grin and began speaking.

"What did he say?" A member of CLUCK Baptist asked. "Turn it up!"

Dorothy did as requested. It didn't help.

"I still don't know what he said," someone else complained."

As everyone leaned forward straining to hear, the problem soon became apparent. The words were in Chinese.

"What the hell!"

"This is a bootleg movie!"

All eyes focused on Connie. She shrugged. "I didn't know!"

"That's what you get when you buy DVDs out of the trunk of a car," Hattie chastised. "And it's not the first time." Praying for Connie's soul took up a lot of Hattie's time. The woman was always up to some kind of foolishness.

Connie didn't argue. "I plead the fifth."

One of the ladies-began to giggle. "It doesn't matter; Denzel looks good even speaking Chinese."

Thelma decided to take advantage of the light mood. "Do some of you remember when the Road Wanderers took that trip to Mackinaw Island?"

Those who had gone on the trip began sharing humorous stories about one of the travel club's most successful ventures. The atmosphere on the bus changed to one of affable camaraderie as the ladies who went on that trip began to trade colorful stories. Hattie, Dorothy and Thelma exchanged smiles that lasted until Mr. Hadley announced that they were turning off the highway at the next exit.

"We've been on the road for a while," he told them. "I need to stretch and eat lunch."

At the stopover, everyone piled off the bus. They were delighted to see that they had a choice of two restaurants.

"Be back on the bus in forty-five minutes," Thelma ordered.

Bea, Connie, Hattie, and Miss Fanny made the same dining choice. They were joined by Dorothy and Thelma. When Dorothy saw their bus driver enter the eatery, she beckoned him to their table. He hesitated, until she called out to him that his meal would be her treat. The others weren't too happy about her generosity.

"Don't feed him," Connie whispered. "I don't like him."

"Me either." Miss Fanny's position on the rude driver had been loudly established.

"I don't think anybody on the bus likes him." Bea had heard the complaints about his discourteous manner, and she agreed.

"Why did you invite him over here?" Hattie had distanced herself from their driver when she asked him if he knew Jesus and he told her that he didn't believe in God. "He's a heathen."

"I want to find out what makes him tick," Dorothy told them, just as the man reached the table and sat down. After everyone ordered, they engaged in small talk.

"This reminds me of the time the Road Wanderers went to St. Louis and we ate at Sweetie Pie's restaurant," said Bea. "My mouth is watering just thinking about it."

"I took a group to Sweetie Pies once," Hadley interjected. "The food was delicious, but the folks on the bus were a pain in the ass. That trip was sort of like this one."

He took another bite of his food, seemingly unaware of the affect his words had on the women at the table. All eyes were on him, and none of them were friendly.

Hattie puffed up. "Young man, watch your language! And what are you saying—that this is not a good trip?"

"I've seen better," he deadpanned.

"I'm sure you've had worse passengers," Thelma snapped defensively.

"Not much." He kept on eating.

Eyes were rolled and scowls appeared on the ladies' faces at that comment. Dorothy pushed her plate aside and turned to him.

"So, Mr. Hadley..."

"Call me George."

"So George, you told Thelma and me that you were an emergency substitute driver for our Mr. Sweeney. What happened to him?"

He stopped eating with his fork half-way to his mouth. "How am I supposed to know? He asked me to fill in for him and I did."

"He asked you to fill in for him?" Thelma looked puzzled. "The dispatcher from the bus company told us that you asked Mr. Sweeney if you could substitute for him because you needed the hours."

"He asked me. I asked him. Whatever! If the dispatcher knows so much about everything, you should ask him what happened to Sweeney."

His manner was so curt that neither Thelma nor Dorothy questioned him further. Hattie had no such reservation.

"You know Mr. Sweeney has been driving the Road Wanderers on our trips for quite a while. He's always been so friendly and polite. What happened in your life to make you so rude?"

The question seemed to amuse Hadley. He chuckled. "Who knows? Maybe it's in my genes, but I've got to tell you I like your style." He winked at her and continued eating.

"Too bad the same can't be said about yours," Miss Fanny countered.

Finished with her meal, Bea sat back and studied the man who had been sent to drive their tour bus. He wasn't bad looking. Of average height, he was clean shaven and wore his hair closely cut, which complemented his square jawed face. She would guess him to be in his forties and if the snug fit of his company uniform was any indication, he was in really good physical shape. There didn't appear to be an ounce of fat on his muscular frame. Despite his unpleasant manner, more than one woman on the bus had given him an appreciative glance. Bea also noticed that the highly polished shoes he wore were from a very expensive men's designer with whom she was familiar. In addition, his nails were manicured. The man was fashion conscious as well as fastidious. *Interesting.*

"How long have you been driving for the bus company?" she queried.

"For a short time."

"Your time might be even shorter on earth if you don't watch that lead foot of yours," Miss Fanny admonished. She didn't like this man and didn't care if he knew it.

"You're the last one to criticize somebody's driving the way you came flying into the church parking lot this morning," Hattie warned her mother-in-law. "You drive like a bat out of hell."

"Just like him," Dorothy said tightly, indicating Hadley.

Thelma lifted a brow. "I wouldn't be surprised if the police wasn't after *both* of you."

Miss Fanny ignored her, but Hadley began choking on the coffee he was drinking. Hattie slapped him on the back until his cough subsided. Without acknowledging her kindness, he rose abruptly.

"I'm outta here. I'll see you all back at the bus." The ladies watched him until he went out the door.

"Doesn't he seem a little odd?" Bea observed.

"No, he *seems* like an ass hole," Dorothy snarled

"I'll second that," said Thelma. "He didn't even thank you for the meal."

"All I'm saying is how many bus drivers do you know get manicures?"

Miss Fanny glared at Bea. "I hope you're not gearing up for one of your detective fantasies. Just because you've got your investigator's license please don't..."

"You've got a license?" Dorothy squealed.

"You're *a real* private investigator?" Thelma looked thrilled.

"Girl, *yes!*" Bea beamed.

"She's going to start an actual detective agency," Hattie informed them proudly.

Connie filled in the blanks. "It'll be called Grandmothers, Incorporated."

"Oh, Lord!" Miss Fanny groaned as she rose to leave. "I hope you fools left that detective mess back in Indianapolis. We've got enough problems on this trip as it is."

"Now, that's the truth," Dorothy agreed.

"Amen," Thelma concurred.

Bea was insulted. "I'm not looking for any trouble."

"And if you don't bring none, there won't be none." Miss Fanny sniffed.

Throwing the money for her tab on the table, she headed toward the door.

CHAPTER 4

"Ladies, may we officially welcome you to Camp Reconciliation."

Thelma spread her arms to indicate the camp-like surroundings in which the women would be spending the next three nights. Her attempt at humor didn't garner a titter.

Hattie looked around the room at the tight faces of the women gathered in the dining hall of the conference center. If body language meant anything, expletives would be flying in a matter of seconds. She prayed that her efforts to do the Lord's work wouldn't be in vain. Thelma and Dorothy were trying so hard to make this whole thing work.

It was Dorothy's turn to attempt to break the ice. "As you can see our accommodations aren't luxurious, but they are comfortable. Obviously, this is the dining area, which can more than accommodate us. The kitchen..." she glanced behind her. "As you see it has a serving window, and commercial stainless steel appliances. We can serve everybody cafeteria style."

"Who's cooking the first meals?" someone from the gathering wanted to know.

Before the trip, each church had agreed to share cooking duties. A budget had been set for each meal, and the ladies attending had submitted their menus. The gesture was meant to be a cooperative effort. Hattie stepped forward.

"Well, the retreat planning committee..."

"Dorothy, Thelma and *you*," someone else called out. It was a reminder that there was resentment that only Mt. Malachi members planned the retreat. Hattie ignored the dig.

"We came up with a schedule and at this time we'll give each of you a copy." The papers were distributed. There was silence as the plans were studied. The former first lady of Mt. Malachi spoke up.

"I see that CLUCK Baptist members will be the first to cook," Lucretia Martin noted coolly.

"We did the meal schedule alphabetically by church names," Thelma explained.

"I guess it is okay if the amateurs go first," she sniffed.

"Uh oh," Connie whispered to Bea. "Sounds like there's going to be a cooking competition."

Dorothy tried to mollify the situation. "Breaking bread together is a wonderful thing. Remember the Last Supper?"

"And we all know how that ended," Miss Fanny quipped.

There was a rumbling of agreement among the women that threatened to erupt into a protest. George Hadley entered the room at that moment pushing a dolly loaded with boxes. He was accompanied by the grounds keeper, Mr. Lucas—who some of the ladies said resembled the character, Barney Fife, on the old Andy Griffith TV series. Mr. Lucas had met them at the main building of the conference center and presented Thelma with the key.

"I live in the town you ladies passed about twenty miles back," he had informed them. "I'll come back in a day or two to check on you."

They had assumed that he had gone on his way, but it looked as though Mr. Hadley had recruited him to help haul in the food supplies they had brought on the trip.

"Where should we put these?" Mr. Hadley asked.

"I know he don't want me to answer that," Angela Rivers mumbled. Indignant, she turned to her mother. "Why do we have to cook? We're supposed to be guests! Mama, I can't believe you agreed to this." Her mother, Ruth, ignored her.

Thelma led Hadley and Mr. Lucas to the kitchen while Dorothy withdrew a stack of envelopes from a folder. She waved them in the air.

"Your room assignments are inside these sealed envelopes. There are numbers on the doors of each room. Even numbers are on the right of the dining hall. Odd numbers are on the left. As your information packets stated, there are four beds to each room."

"And we will get the roommates we requested, right?" someone asked.

Dorothy swallowed. *How could she phrase this?* "We did the best we could. Now, to expedite things, we're asking you not to open your envelopes until you step into the hallway."

As the names were called, she enjoyed the brief moments of tranquility because she knew that very soon all hell was going to break loose.

****

As Connie walked down the hallway to her room, she was glad that Bea, Hattie and she had agreed not to put each other's names as roommate preferences. They spent enough time together. She wanted to experience the element of surprise when she stepped across the threshold, and that she did.

"Hello!" came a cheerful greeting from a bird-like looking woman perched on the bed closest to the door. "I'm Pearl Mason." She flashed Connie a warm smile.

Connie returned her smile with one equally as gracious. "I'm Connie Palmer."

The woman sitting on the bed next to Pearl introduced herself as Ruth Rivers. Short and rotund, she appeared to be in her seventies and wore her gray and white mixed hair in braids pinned across the top of her head. Connie hadn't seen that hairstyle since her late grandmother wore it back in rural Tennessee.

"This is my daughter, Angela Rivers." Ruth nodded to the younger woman putting her belongings in the night stand drawer next to her bed.

Angela was an attractive woman. She was plump and shapely, with a curly hair style that complemented her pretty, round face. She nodded a silent greeting to their new roommate.

"Hope you don't mind the bed by the window," Pearl told Connie.

"Not at all." Connie rolled her small travel case across the solid wood floor to the steel framed twin bed. Although the front entrance hall that greeted them at this isolated conference center was impressive, the sleeping accommodations were spartan. The beds were covered with matching plain cotton bedspreads. Plopping down on the mattress Connie discovered that it was as hard as a rock.

"This is going to be interesting," she grimaced.

Angela pounded her own mattress with her fist. "I'm going to need a chiropractor after this."

"That makes two of us." Connie began to unpack.

There were small metal closets opposite each bed. When she opened hers she was glad to see that it had hangers.

"Oh, Connie," Pearl's singsong voice drifted from across the room. "I forgot to mention that the three of us are members of Twelve Disciples Community. Which church do you belong to?"

"I attend CLUCK Baptist sometimes and sometimes I attend Mt. Malachi."

Ruth Rivers raised a brow. "Yes, dear, but you're a member of *which* congregation, CLUCK Baptist or Mt. Malachi?"

"Neither one. Most of the time I don't go to church."

Preoccupied with her task, Connie didn't notice that all action in the room had ceased. She looked up to see all eyes were on her.

"You're not baptized?" There was incredulity in Pearl's inquiry.

Connie resumed unpacking. "I was baptized when I was a child in Tennessee. I just don't go to church regularly." She didn't feel it necessary to explain her actions.

"So you're looking for a church home." Angela concluded.

Connie couldn't help but notice the hopeful inflection in her voice. Too bad she had to disappoint her. "No, I'm not."

"We'll see, dear," Pearl assured her sweetly. "We'll see."

There was a predatory smile on the woman's face as Pearl Mason looked at her as though she had the word *convert* stamped across her forehead.

Inwardly, Connie groaned. *Oh Lord! I'm now a candidate for saving.* The gleam in Pearl's eyes was a telltale sign.

In the room occupied by Fanny Collier, attempts at civility were tenuous at best. As far as Miss Fanny was concerned, the pairing of the women in this room was a formula for disaster.

Besides herself, there was Viola Smith, a member of Twelve Disciples, a lifelong friend of Hattie and Bea as well as the biggest gossip in Indianapolis. Telling other people's business was Viola's passion, and she would indulge in it anytime, anywhere and about anybody. Worse than that, her percentage of accuracy about her chosen subjects was close to zero. She never got anything right.

Their third roommate was Autumn Randall, the wife of the pastor of CLUCK Baptist and an ongoing victim of Viola's scandal-mongering. Strikingly beautiful, the tall, slender young woman had the dubious distinction of being the pastor's second wife. She had replaced the much loved first Mrs. Randall, who after her death had been elevated to near sainthood by members of the church. Autumn's stunning looks, her flair for fashion and the fact that she was twenty-five years younger than the fifty something year old minister, made her life difficult in the church community. Added to that was the fact that the Reverend had married the woman less than a year after the first Mrs. Randall's demise. Eyebrows were still being raised about that.

The last bed in the room was occupied by Lucretia Martin. Like Miss Fanny, she was a member of Mt. Malachi Baptist. If it was anyone else in her church Miss Fanny would have been delighted, but she and Lucretia were like oil and water. It was no secret that they didn't like each other. Why in the world the two of them had been put in the same room she didn't know! There would be no reconciliation here.

The irony was that Lucretia and Miss Fanny had known each other for decades and they had more in common than anyone else in this room. Both were widows and they had served on many church committees together and gotten along well. That is until Reverend Trees replaced Lucretia's late husband as pastor and became interested in Miss Fanny's daughter-in-law. Lucretia had been acting as pseudo first lady of their church since her husband's death, and she felt threatened by Hattie. It was then that the former first lady began to wage a silent vendetta against her, criticizing and putting her down at every opportunity.

Out of respect for her age and former position in the church, Hattie ignored the woman's actions, but Miss Fanny did not. She resented Lucretia's displays of self-importance and the battle between the two began.

As the four roommates moved around silently putting their things away, Miss Fanny and Lucretia cut their eyes at each other, neither having forgotten their numerous run-ins past or present. Miss Fanny was grateful that there were two beds between them, but even that was too close.

Finished with her unpacking, she settled on the bed, put her feet up, and adjusted the flattened pillow behind her back. Leaning against the headboard, Miss Fanny watched the others as they moved around the room.

Lord! What a weekend this was going to be. She was trapped in this room with a gossip, a diva, and a cow! How lucky could she get?

Bea stood in the doorway of the room she was to occupy and couldn't believe what she was seeing. How could Dorothy and Thelma have dared assign her to be roommates with LaVerne Nelson, Rosemary Sanders *and* Ethel Pramby? Three women she couldn't stand! There was no way this was happening and she made her objection to the arrangement loud and clear.

"Hellllll no!"

Three pairs of eyes cut her to the quick. Ethel Pramby tossed a sharp retort to Bea's retreating back. "You got that right."

Stalking the halls like a lioness on the hunt, Bea checked rooms until she found the one that Dorothy and Thelma were sharing. To her surprise Hattie was in there too. She was unpacking and looked quite content. That was about to end!

With hand on her hip, Bea gave all three women a murderous look as she let her overnight bag fall to the floor with a thud.

Thelma and Dorothy were the first to react. Gauging her demeanor, they were smart enough to avoid eye contact. Hattie, on the other hand wasn't. She feigned ignorance.

"Hi, Bea, is there a problem?"

The hard gleam in her friend's eyes caused Hattie's smile to falter, but she quickly regained her bravado. Bea had threatened to do her harm so many times she couldn't count them, but she was still here.

Hattie's nonchalance only served to agitate Bea further. Her eyes narrowed into mere slits and the muscles in her face started to twitch. She was so mad she could spit nails, as she returned her attention to Dorothy and Thelma.

"I'm going to ignore Little Miss Sunshine, and ask the two of you how could you do this to me?" Crossing the threshold, Bea's voice rose. "You put me in the room with The Devils of Darkness! Are you insane?"

"Bea...I...I...know that you're upset..." Thelma stuttered.

"And we know you can't stand them," Dorothy croaked.

"*But*," Hattie added calmly, "the point of this retreat *is* learning how to get along."

"Besides," Thelma pointed an accusatory finger at Hattie. "It was her idea to put you with the evil triplets!"

Bea whirled on Hattie. "Your idea! What kind of friend are you?"

Hattie remained unfazed by Bea's wrath. "One who is trying to do the right thing."

"Well you damn well better do the right thing by *me!*"

Following the source of the angry declaration, the women looked over to see Ethel Pramby standing in the doorway, suitcase in hand. She was as upset as Bea.

"I absolutely refuse to stay in the same room with a woman who helped put my friend, Charmaine Schaffer in jail."

"Her name is *Charlie Mae*, and she's not in jail because of me," Bea Bell reminded her. "The jail bird embezzled investment money and got caught. Maybe birds of a feather stick together."

Short in stature and as thin as a rail, Ethel looked as though she couldn't do battle with a flea, but from her stance, the sixty something year old woman was ready to spar. Bea had never had a physical altercation in her life, but if this combative big mouth was ready to take her on she would be making her professional wrestling debut today.

Ethel stepped into the room. Dorothy, Thelma and Hattie stood poised for trouble.

Ethel took a step toward Bea. "First you tried to steal her husband…"

"They were separated…"

"Then you and your meddling friends had the police on Charmaine's case about her husband's death."

"*Charlie Mae* wasn't concerned about his death that was for sure…"

"Now you've got the nerve to stand here and insult me?"

The five foot two inch Bea and the barely five foot Ethel were face to face. They might be fairly matched in height, but Bea knew that her one hundred and fifty plus pounds gave her the weight advantage. She was ready to take her down, but her friends weren't having it. Dorothy stepped between them, Thelma held Ethel back. Hattie concentrated on Bea. Noise from the bickering duo had brought curious spectators to the door. The trio tried to calm the brewing storm.

"Stop you two!"

"Get back, Ethel!"

"You're better than this, Bea." Hattie declared.

Bea and Ethel continued to exchange wicked glares, but both took a step back. Thelma released her grip on Ethel while Hattie went to close the door on the unwanted spectators. She returned to the combative duo.

"Ya'll ought to be ashamed of yourselves," she reprimanded. "This is a disgrace!"

"I feel like calling this whole thing off and taking that bus back to Indianapolis," said Dorothy.

Thelma nodded. "I'm with you. Nothing like this has ever happened on one of our trips before. What are you two trying to do, put us out of business? We can't have brawling on our road trips."

"Well what did you expect?" Ethel snapped. "You're the ones who put us in the same room! Any idiot knows you gotta take small steps before you take big ones!"

"Our thoughts exactly, but *somebody* assured us that everything would be okay." Thelma turned an accusing eye on Hattie.

"We are doing the Lord's work here," Hattie insisted.

"Then let Him stay in the room with *her*," Ethel spat.

Bea started to react, but Hattie intervened. "No, I'll do it. If everybody agrees, I'll move into the room with Bea, Rosemary and LaVerne. Ethel can take my place in here."

Bea had another suggestion. "Why don't *I* stay in here with Dorothy and Thelma and *you* take my place in the room with the other three."

Thinking quickly, Hattie countered. "Because the two of us together might soften the hearts of those sisters in Christ. I'd feel privileged doing the Lord's work with you."

"Oh, please." Bea knew that Hattie's words were code for: *I'm not about to move in with those two she-devils alone.* She opened her mouth to object, but a sudden thought stopped her. It might be fun seeing The Angel of Mercy trying to practice what she preached.

"You know, I'll take you up on that, Hattie. Since this roommate idea was yours in the first place you deserve what you get."

"Then it's settled." Ethel strutted to the bed formerly occupied by Hattie, kicked off her shoes and settled in the middle of it. Crossing her arms and her ankles, her body language dared anyone to object.

Thelma and Dorothy exchanged a knowing look. Ethel Pramby was often called the 'pit bull' by those who knew her. It looked like they were about to find out why. Their eyes slid back to Hattie.

"Yeah, you do deserve what you get," Thelma gritted between clenched teeth.

"But I don't know why *we* have to suffer," Dorothy eyed Ethel.

"Okay, Hattie, pack your stuff," Bea demanded. "You've got some lost souls to save."

CHAPTER 5

Bea stood in the conference center kitchen and watched as the large pan of biscuits was taken out of the oven. They were golden brown and light as a feather. She knew that for a fact, because it was her own special recipe, and the ladies at the retreat couldn't seem to get enough.

There was no need to be modest about it, but the ladies of CLUCK Baptist—Ethel, Rosemary, LaVerne and Autumn—had exceeded all expectations. They had prepared the first meal for the retreat and the bar they had managed to set for those coming after them was very high. In a unanimous compliment to the cooks, the attendees had eaten every morsel.

Tension was high when the women first entered the kitchen. As the pastor's wife, Autumn Randall took it on herself to try and serve as mediator between the battling church members. The mutual animosity between Bea, Ethel, Rosemary and LaVerne was so well known, that it was the pastor of their church who had personally made the request that each woman sign up for the Reconciliation Retreat. His young wife was doing her best to make certain that the members in their contingent got along. Her cheerful disposition was in stark contrast to the surliness of the others in the kitchen. She had volunteered to cook the main dish, baked chicken. There was doubt about her ability to handle the responsibility. Nobody at CLUCK Baptist knew whether Autumn could cook, and they didn't want to take any chances.

All doubts faded when the First Lady of CLUCK Baptist reached into her pocket and withdrew a plastic pouch filled with her own special spices. She was serious about preparing this meal, and the result was a succulent work of art.

Dinner was served cafeteria style and the consensus from the attendees was that the meal was superb. The ladies of CLUCK Baptist were ecstatic.

While everyone was dining, Autumn announced that she was going for a walk.

"But it's getting dark," Bea warned. "I've heard that it gets pitch black in these woods."

Autumn seemed unconcerned. "I'll be okay." She exited through the kitchen door.

"I guess she's tired of us," Laverne sniffed.

"Who wouldn't be?" Bea shot back. She understood the young woman's need to get away from the others. These ladies were a challenge.

After dinner, Thelma and Dorothy led an information session. Hattie sat on the sidelines ready to offer assistance if needed. Lord knows the women on this retreat were a handful. There wasn't a thing they didn't complain about—the driver drove too fast, their bedrooms were too small, the beds were lumpy—the complaints went on and on.

The camaraderie shared by the retreat attendees at dinner time totally disappeared during the general meeting. It was like a Cold War in the dining room. Dorothy and Thelma were like soldiers in the heat of battle, dodging bullets at every turn.

"Tell us again why you two are the only ones with cell phones?" someone wanted to know.

"Everyone here agreed that we would be out of contact with the outside world while we're here," Dorothy reiterated patiently. "We want to communicate with each other without distractions."

"Our telephones are for emergencies." Thelma couldn't count the times this explanation had been given.

"I thought this conference center would at least have a telephone," one person noted.

"If you read your information packet, it says that it doesn't." Dorothy's patience was waning. "We will use our cell phones if we need to make calls."

"But it's dark out here. I didn't know it was going to be this dark," another person said in a childlike whimper.

"What's that got to do with us having cell phones?" Thelma wanted to know.

"Haven't you seen those movies where zombies, killers and such come out of the dark on nights like this?" Angela Rivers looked out one of the multitude of dining room windows into the blackness. "I thought some lights were supposed to come on outside automatically when it got dark."

"Yeah," Ruth Rivers grumbled. "Where are the lights..."

"And the curtains or blinds?" Ethel Pramby asked. "Anybody could be peeking through those windows."

A chorus of nervous whispers swept through the room.

"I'm sure they'll come on." Dorothy wanted to reassure them, but they were right. It was quite dark and the lights should have come on by now. She glanced at Thelma who came to her aid.

"We'll call Mr. Lucas if they don't come on soon."

That wasn't enough for Miss Fanny. "When? After we're all dead in our beds! Did somebody lock that front door up there? Do our bedroom doors have locks?"

Hattie shot her mother-in-law a look that would kill. That old lady could throw a damper on the Second Coming.

The voices of concern became louder as suggestions were made to put newspaper over the dining room windows to hide the dark.

"You can't even see the stars through those trees." Lucretia Martin scowled, peering through the window into the darkness.

Dorothy had had enough. "Oh be quiet, Lucretia!" she barked before turning on the others. "I am sick and tired of all of ya'll. You've been whining and nagging and complaining since we left Indianapolis, and I'm through hearing it! Now look at your agendas and shut up!"

Stunned by her outburst, the women sat in shocked surprise. Even Thelma was caught off guard.

"D...D...Dorothy," she stuttered, not sure about what to say. She looked at Hattie who seemed just as shell-shocked.

Hoping to save the day, Hattie started to rise, go to the front and help diffuse the situation. Dorothy had another idea.

"Sit down, Hattie! I don't need your help."

Hattie plopped back down in her seat. Just as expected the room erupted in loud protest.

"I know you're not disrespecting me, Dorothy Riggs!"

"Who do you think you are?"

"We're not some of those children you used to boss around!"

"You're not talking to me like that!"

Women were on their feet with hands on hips, and fingers wagging at Dorothy, Thelma and Hattie. Thelma didn't seem sure how to respond to the turmoil. Hattie shot out of her chair ready to verbally defend herself.

Dorothy ignored all the comments and began to read the agenda loudly, adding to the din. An ear piercing shriek reverberated throughout the room. "Quiet!"

Everybody's eyes turned in the direction of the sound. Autumn Randall stood in the kitchen doorway.

"What is going on in here?" she demanded.

Thelma had a question of her own. "Where in the world have you been?"

"I went for a walk and I could hear the noise all the way outside!"

"I can't believe that you were out there in the dark." Hattie looked at the younger woman as though she had lost her mind.

Autumn held up a pocket sized flashlight. "I managed to find my way back."

"How did you get in?" Miss Fanny wanted to know. "I thought all the doors were locked?"

"I came in through the kitchen door. It was still unlocked from when I went out of it."

Miss Fanny wasn't happy with that answer. "Okay, who's responsible for security around here?"

"That's it! I'm tired of all of this grumbling and complaining!" Dorothy bellowed. "Everybody go to your rooms and go to bed right now. We start early tomorrow with a hike in the woods."

"I don't think so," Ethel disagreed.

Dorothy ignored her. "Tomorrow when I call over the loudspeaker for everyone to get up I expect you to do just that."

"Or what?" Lucretia challenged.

"You'll find out." Thelma was tired of these women too. She rose and started walking out of the dining room.

"Now read your agendas and we'll see you tomorrow! Come on, Dorothy. This meeting is over."

Amid the barrage of protests, Hattie joined the women in their walkout, praising Dorothy and Thelma for their tough stance, but having to agree with one of the complaints.

"They act like a bunch of whining babies, but I think that they're right about the outdoor lights. It does look spooky out there without them. If they don't come on you'd better call Mr. Lucas and tell him to get over here and fix them."

"We can't do that," said Dorothy. "After we got here, I discovered that I left my cell phone at the church in the bag with the DVDs."

"You're kidding! But Thelma, you have your phone don't you?"

"Yeah, I have one, but the battery is dead and I forgot the charger. It's at home."

"Oh, my Lord! What if something happens? What are you going to do?" Hattie's concern was obvious.

Dorothy and Thelma exchanged a look, before Dorothy shrugged.

"We don't have a clue. Let's pray that we don't have an emergency this weekend."

CHAPTER 6

"Ladies! I want to thank CLUCK Baptist for that marvelous meal they cooked last night."

"What the hell? " Bea startled awake as the strident voice rang out over the loud speaker.

A groggy Rosemary Sanders propped herself on her elbows. "Is that Dorothy hollering at us again?"

It was, and she continued.

"I'm trying to be patient and it would be nice if every church present had a chance to show off their cooking skills. We, the ladies from Mt. Malachi are trying to do that this morning as we *attempt* to cook breakfast. But in order to do that we need *COOKING UTENSILS!*" she barked the last two words, making it clear that she was angry. "Every knife in this damn kitchen is missing. I want those knives returned *immediately*."

"That woman has lost her natural born mind!" said LaVerne Nelson as she squinted through sleep glazed eyes at the clock on the wooden night stand. "It's six o'clock in the morning!"

Rosemary was on her feet putting her robe on. "I'm going to go give her a piece of *my* mind!"

"I'm going with you," Laverne declared.

Bea looked over at Hattie, but her bed was empty. She didn't have to guess where she was. Putting on her robe and slippers, she followed the others out of the room. They were not alone. By the time everyone reached the dining room, it was already filled with irate, women complaining about having been awakened at dawn by Dorothy's theatrics.

As Bea suspected, Hattie was with Dorothy and Thelma engaged in a heated discussion with some of the enraged attendees.

"It was all that foolish talk about vampires and murderers that scared everybody!" Ethel Pramby was telling the trio.

Dorothy wasn't moved. "I don't care! Even the butter knives are missing. We need those knives!"

"How are we supposed to eat breakfast?" Hattie gripped. "With forks?"

"With our fingers if we have to."

"We don't need knives to eat."

"Did you expect us to sleep out here in the wilderness with no protection?" LaVerne wanted to know.

Thelma was exasperated. "This is *not* the wilderness. We are in a wooded area, in comfortable lodgings and there are people who know where we are."

"Maybe if we exercised a little more faith we wouldn't need knives for protection," Hattie suggested.

"I'm not happy about being shouted awake at the crack of dawn" said Connie, "But Hattie is right. We need the knives for practical purposes. Anyway, you should never bring a knife to a gun fight." She winked at Hattie who looked at her suspiciously.

"Are you packing?"

"Is the pope Catholic?"

Hattie sighed in disgust. "You've got no shame. This is a Christian gathering..."

"Can we get back on the subject?" Dorothy growled. "If you want to eat this morning, I want those knives. We've got sausage to slice and butter to spread. Then we're going hiking and communing with God!" With that she stormed into the kitchen.

Most of the knives were returned to the kitchen and the ladies of Mt. Malachi finally prepared breakfast. The meal was heartily consumed.

****

The day dawned crisp and clear with the sun peeking through the trees. The air was fresh with only a slight breeze. The morning's agenda called for a nature hike and there could not have been a more perfect day to do so.

Dorothy, Thelma, and Hattie were the assigned leaders for the trek. They were huddled together in the yard outside the conference center checking their trail maps. The ladies milled around waiting impatiently for directions.

"Somebody tell me why we're out here walking this early?" Ethel Pramby said loudly, addressing no one in particular. "Nobody said a thing about stumbling around in the woods in the cold."

"We need to find out how to reach that river that runs through the park," Hattie explained trying to generate a sliver of interest among the ladies about their forthcoming hike. "There are three different hiking trails, showcasing different points of interest and they all end at a beautiful waterfall. Ladies, this is going to be a day you won't soon forget."

"I'd like to," someone grumbled.

"Today's hike is a chance to bond," Thelma explained. "The goal is to clear our heads and our hearts as we walk together in harmony."

"I think that's a good idea," Autumn Randall agreed amiably.

"Where exactly are we walking to?" Connie asked.

"Deadman's Falls," Thelma pointed to the little blue star on the map mounted on the front of the conference building. "It's right in the middle of the park."

"And we heard its beautiful this time of year," Hattie said enthusiastically.

"How far is that?" Bea had been going to a gym lately, but she wasn't exactly an exercise buff. "It looks like a good distance to me."

"It's only a two mile hike," Thelma said brightly.

"Two miles there and *back*?" Angela Rivers was one of the youngest women present, but it was obvious from her round build that she didn't do a lot of walking. Judging by the rumble emanating from the other ladies it was apparent that she wasn't the only one.

"I'm not sure I can make it that far." Connie hadn't anticipated anything like this when she decided to come along. "Maybe I should stay here." Hattie made a move to quash the impending rebellion.

"Ladies! Ladies! "We know it sounds like a challenge, but trust me, we'll be there before you know it." Her words were met with sullen stares. Thelma took over.

"There are three trails leading to the falls. We're going to divide into three groups with Dorothy, Hattie and me each leading one."

"And we've already assigned you to groups, so don't ask," Dorothy warned.

"We'll meet up at the falls, feast on the snacks we brought for you and engage in a discussion about Christians loving one another," said Hattie.

"That sounds nice," stated Pearl Mason from Twelve Disciples. "And at a time like this I feel music is the best way to express our feelings. I'm volunteering to sing a couple of songs along the trail and when we get to the falls to get us in the loving spirit."

There was dead silence which Pearl took to mean that the ladies were grateful for her gracious offer. A slow, satisfied smile spread across her face.

Connie whispered to Bea. "You're going to have to knock me over the head and drag me on that trail if she starts singing." Like the other women present, she had heard Pearl's vocal efforts and was less than impressed.

Hattie, Dorothy and Thelma exchanged looks that clearly indicated that listening to Pearl's caterwauling was not what they had envisioned. Thelma handed out the group assignments. As expected most of the women weren't happy about them, but the group leaders refused to discuss their decisions.

"Let's go," Hattie said hurriedly as soon as she got her list. She was anxious to leave before Pearl was reassigned to her group.

****

Hattie's assembly hadn't gone half a mile and the griping among her fellow hikers had been nonstop.

"My feet hurt."

"You didn't say nothing about rocks being on this trail."

"Is that poison ivy over there?"

"We're walking too fast!"

"I got to pee."

"It's cold out here."

"How much farther?'

"Are bears in these woods?"

"I only wish," Bea muttered to herself. She'd had enough. "These heifers are getting on my last nerve!" She, Hattie and Connie were walking together at the front of the line.

"They're a handful." Connie couldn't deny that. "But you've got to admit seeing this group trying to traipse through these woods is better than a reality show."

Hattie glowered at her. "You're really enjoying all of this falling apart on me, aren't you?"

Connie tried to hold her laughter, but failed. "I'm sorry, Hattie, but this whole thing is funny."

Hattie was annoyed by her lack of empathy. "I'm glad you think so. I don't."

"Oh, can it! I know you didn't think they weren't going to complain." Bea bent to pick up a large limb to use as a walking stick. "That's all they've been doing since we got on the bus." Examining the wood in her hand, she thought seriously of using it as a weapon.

"What we're trying to do here is Christianity at work," Hattie insisted.

Connie looked skeptical. "It looks like the devil's winning so far."

Hattie was appalled. "Connie, that's blasphemous! Lord, have mercy! No matter how hard I try to help, you're determined to keep knocking on the gates of hell."

"So are they." Connie indicated the women behind them.

A loud noise from the woods stopped all conversation. The hikers froze.

"What was that?" Bea looked worried.

"I don't know." Like the others, Connie strained to listen. "It sounds like shouting."

Everyone remained motionless. The sound seemed to come from their left, deep in the woods. Nobody stirred, until a panic stricken voice came from the back of the line.

"Where's Gladys? She was behind me."

Mentally, Hattie counted the number of hikers. A member of Twelve Disciples, Gladys Hodges was a quiet, unassuming woman in her fifties who was one of the less annoying women on the retreat. She had been the last one in the line of hikers, but she was no longer there. Hattie began shouting.

"Gladys!"

The others joined her in the effort as the sound of Gladys' name interrupted the serenity of their surroundings. It didn't take long for their fellow hiker to stumble out of the woods from the vicinity of where the noise had been heard. The ladies hurried to her.

"Where in the world have you been?" Hattie demanded, feeling both aggravated and relieved. "I said we had to stick together."

"I know, but I said I had to pee. I ducked into the woods to take care of business, but after I finished, I couldn't find the trail. So, I started yelling. Didn't ya'll hear me?"

"We heard something, but you should have told somebody what you were doing and not gone off alone," Hattie chastised. *Would these women ever learn?*

"Weren't you scared?' asked Angela.

Gladys nodded. "I was until I saw that I wasn't far from the road we came on. Before I heard ya'll calling me I was headed that way toward the bus to see if I could get some help."

"What bus?" Hattie was getting antsy. They were wasting time.

"The one we came to this retreat on. It's parked by the side of the road right over there."

Hattie sighed impatiently. "What are you talking about, Gladys? It can't be. The driver's not coming back for us until Sunday."

Gladys pointed in the direction from which she came. "The bus we came here on is parked right over there, through those trees."

"I'm sure it's not our bus," said Hattie, anxious to make up for the time that they'd lost. She glanced at her watch. "We've got to get going. We've wasted enough time." She turned to walk back down the trail.

Gladys stood firm. "I'm telling you, that what I saw through those trees over there was *our* bus. I recognize the color and the company name written on it." There was not a hint of doubt in her voice.

The ladies all looked at Hattie, waiting for an explanation. She emitted an exasperated growl.

"Don't look at me! If it is our bus, I don't know why it's here. I thought the driver left yesterday."

"Well, one good way to find out if it's really ours is to go see," Bea suggested.

"But we'll be the last ones at the water fall!' Hattie wailed. The other hikers ignored her and followed Gladys who retraced her steps.

"Come on, Hattie," Connie tossed over her shoulder as she followed the others. "Aren't you curious?"

"No!" Hattie was adamant. "We're gonna be late!"

Her words fell on deaf ears as all the women who had been complaining about every tree, twig and bug in the woods left the trail to thrash through the bushes.

"Maybe we can get a ride back to the conference center," somebody said happily.

"Or home to Indianapolis."

Hattie wanted to scream. Instead, with a sigh of resignation the group leader turned and followed the others. The trek to the bus wasn't far.

"Well, I'll be dammed!" Connie came to an abrupt halt just behind Gladys. There was no mistaking the vehicle parked off the road as being their tour bus.

"What did I tell you?" Gladys glanced triumphantly around the group of hikers. Some of them were very happy to see a source of transportation.

"Hallelujah! Let's get a ride back to the cabin."

"I'll be happy just to sit down and get off my feet."

Bea pushed her way to the front of the group. "Hold on everybody. I want to know why the bus is here. Maybe it broke down."

Hattie was incredulous. "You mean that fool driver's been sitting here since yesterday? Why didn't he call for help?"

"Or walk back to the center," Connie added.

Determined to find answers, Bea strode up to the bus doors which were partially open. She pushed on them and they parted easily. Cautiously, she climbed aboard. The sunlight streaming through the interior onto the cushioned seats of the empty bus gave it an eerie glow as her eyes spotted the unimaginable. George Hadley, the obnoxious driver with whom she and her friends had been sharing a meal only 24 hours ago, was laying face down in the narrow aisle. A large butcher knife was protruding from his back. The scream she tried to emit stuck in her throat.

Instinctively, Bea backed away, colliding with Hattie who had followed her on to the bus.

"Hey, watch it. Do you see the bus...?" The rest of the words went unspoken as she stared in disbelief at the gruesome sight.

Baffled by the behavior of her two friends, an impatient Connie boarded the bus.

"What's going on in here?" Her eyes traveled from her two speechless friends to the lifeless body. The scream that had eluded Bea and Hattie tore from her throat with such force the birds in the nearby trees scattered. All three women hurried from the bus interior, nearly tripping over each other in their scramble to exit.

"What in the world is wrong?" Gladys wanted to know.

Hattie blurted, "The driver is dead!"

CHAPTER 7

Gladys looked skeptical. She took a step forward. "Oh come on now, Hattie. We just saw the man yesterday."

Although shaken, Bea took charge. "I'm sorry to break the news to all of you, but the driver *is* dead." There were shocked gasps.

"Oh no!

"What happened?"

"Was it a heart attack?'

"No!" Connie was trembling. "He's in there lying on the floor with a knife sticking out of his back." Her voice broke.

Anguish was quickly replaced by fear. Still there was some denial.

"Are you *sure* he didn't just have a heart attack?" one woman asked.

"There's a big ass knife sticking out of his back," Bea said testily. "I think we can rule out natural causes."

"We're all going to be murdered out here!" someone shrieked.

Hysteria began to take hold. Some of the women started crying. Hattie joined hands with a few women and began to pray.

Connie fought her own rising hysterics. "We are *not* going to be murdered. The first thing we need to do is contact the police."

"No," Hattie countered. "The first thing we need to do is get out of here!"

There was general agreement. Taking control of her own fear, Bea spoke up.

"I think you're right, but before we do that I need to go back on that bus."

"What?" Hattie was horrified. "Why?"

"Evidence." Bea headed toward the opened bus doors. Connie caught her by the arm.

"Bea, this is a *real* body, a *real* murder."

"Ain't it the truth!" a consenting voice rang out.

"This is no time for you to play detective," warned Bea's adversarial roommate, Laverne.

There was a chorus of anxious agreement. Offended, Bea looked at the women steadily.

"I *am* a detective and I have the credentials to prove it." To the ardent protests of her fellow hikers, she started to board the bus.

This time it was Hattie who detained her. "What if the killer is still in there?" she whispered anxiously. "Maybe he's hiding between the seats or in the bathroom."

"Perhaps my friends would like to come aboard with me so I'll know somebody has my back," Bea looked pointedly at Hattie and at Connie. Her two comrades didn't appear to be too enthused with her suggestion, but they reluctantly agreed.

To everyone's surprise, except her two best friends, Connie pulled a small .22 handgun out of her jacket pocket. One of the hikers sighed with relief.

"Thank the Lord somebody's got some fire power."

"I wasn't coming to these woods without some." With the skill of a pro, Connie clicked the safety and put a bullet in the chamber.

"Okay, Bea, let's go."

Cautiously, the three women stepped aboard the bus. For a moment they stood in a tight knot at the entrance gathering their courage. Bea stepped forward.

A trail of blood had snaked its way from the knife's entry point down the driver's back. Burrowing in her pocket to produce a tissue, she bent and used it to touch the blood stain.

"What are you doing?" Hattie screeched.

Bea examined the tissue. "The blood is gelled," she declared. "It's my guess he's been dead a while, so I doubt if the killer is still on this bus."

"You don't know that." Hattie's eyes anxiously swept the vehicle's interior.

"Hattie, you check the radio system and see if it's working. Maybe we can get some help here. Come on, Connie," Bea ordered, gingerly stepping over the body.

Trying to ignore the pungent smell of blood, Connie looked away from the corpse as she trailed Bea with her weapon poised and ready. Hattie plopped down in the driver's seat and began fiddling with the communication system, all the while keeping a nervous eye on her friends as they diligently searched between the seats. When the women reached the bathroom, Bea quickly snatched the door open while Connie stood poised to fire. The stall was empty.

"Are you able to get out to anybody?" Bea asked, returning to the front of the bus.

"I can't make head or tails of this contraption," Hattie reported, throwing her hands up in resignation.

Both Bea and Connie groaned at that bit of news.

"I know I don't know anything about these kind of radios," Connie admitted.

Bea shook her head, "Me either."

All three of the women jumped, startled, as one of the hikers banged on the side of the bus and yelled, "What you doing in there?"

Satisfied that no one was aboard, the trio wasted no time exiting the bus to inform the group.

"Except for the body, the bus is empty," Bea relayed.

"Then let's start back to the conference center," Gladys suggested.

Bea countered. "No! First, we need a phone to call the police. There's a radio on board but we can't figure out how to work it. We've got to get to Dorothy and Thelma so they can call for help. We don't know where that man's murderer might be. That means none of us are safe out here in the open. We need to get to the waterfall ASAP and warn the others."

There was a consensus that Bea was right. As Hattie hurried along with the others to the meeting point, she knew that this was not the time or the place to mention that there were no cell phones to make the call.

****

"This is one of the most beautiful spots I've ever seen." Autumn Randall stood in the open meadow across from the waterfall where all of the hikers were to meet. Both Dorothy and Thelma's groups had reached their destination. Everyone was now waiting for Hattie's group to arrive.

Viola Smith's thick eyebrows arched upward. If it were possible to earn a living from gossip, she would be a wealthy woman. Lately, the marriage of Pastor Randall to his much younger second wife had been the focus of most of her gossip mongering. She considered herself an expert on the subject of the Randalls and she was quick to respond to Autumn's observation.

"Really? I heard that you and your husband had a pretty exotic honeymoon. Surely you've been someplace more scenic than this." Without giving Autumn a chance to respond she continued innocently. "Yes, my guess is that you're a woman who makes up her mind pretty quick. How long was it after his wife died that ya'll got married? Less than a year wasn't it?"

A couple of the ladies from the other churches giggled. The CLUCK Baptist contingent wasn't amused.

"Viola!" Thelma warned.

"You couldn't wait to start some shit, could you Viola?" Dorothy growled.

Turning smoothly from the waterfall, Autumn addressed the concerns. "It's all right. I'm sure Viola is just curious." She flashed her nemesis a sinister smile. "And we all *know* what happened to the curious cat."

An indignant Viola was about to respond when the sound of Hattie's group charging up the hiking trail drew everyone's attention. It was obvious that something was wrong. The women looked frazzled and frightened.

"What's the matter?" Dorothy and Thelma asked simultaneously.

Everyone from Hattie's group began talking at once.

"We got to get out of here."

"We're all going to die..."

"It was awful..."

Somehow through the frenzied chatter the message got through to the others that the bus driver was dead. All three groups were panic-stricken. The screeching, crying and lamenting was deafening. Once again, Bea took control.

"Everybody shut up!" she bellowed above the noise. When she was sure she had the women's attention, she continued. "Yes, the bus driver *is* dead. We found the bus parked on a road in the woods with his body on it. He's been stabbed."

"We came to warn everybody," Hattie told them breathlessly.

"There's safety in numbers," Gladys offered. "That way we can see the murderer before he sneaks up on us."

Pearl looked at Connie. "We do have some protection. Connie has a gun."

"And I know how to use it," Connie confirmed. Immediately, the attention of the women shifted in her direction.

"We've got to get back to the ladies at the center and warn them," said Hattie.

Thelma looked scared. "I know you're right, but that means that we'll have to go back through the woods."

"Yeah," Pearl looked equally stricken. "Connie's got a gun, but what do the rest of us have to protect ourselves?"

Immediately hands reached into jackets, backpacks and fanny packs, producing over a dozen kitchen knives that glinted in the sunlight.

"Well I'll be damned!" Dorothy muttered under her breath. "I knew all of those knives wasn't back in that kitchen."

Other women searched the ground for sturdy sticks or large rocks to be used as weapons. In no time, everyone was armed.

"Let somebody try to mess with us now," one of the women declared.

Bea tried to give a pep talk. "Okay ladies, let's get back to the conference center. We'll be safer there than out

here in the open. It will be easier to defend ourselves.
Now I'm going to..."

The rest of her words were lost as shouts went up.

"She's right!"

"Let's get back to the center."

Within seconds, Bea, Connie and Hattie found themselves standing in the clearing alone as the women stampeded like a herd of buffalo back down the trail. The three friends looked at each other.

"What do we do now, Sherlock?" Connie asked.

Bea gave a grim smile. "We're going to do what we do best. Ladies, we have a crime to solve."

CHAPTER 8

Miss Fanny was sitting propped up in the middle of her bed wondering what had possessed her to sign up for this god-awful retreat. She was too old to be up in these woods in the middle of Lord knows where. Besides it was boring. All these cackling hens did was gossip and snipe at each other. She could be home now doing something important. She wasn't sure what, but it had to be better than this.

Of course, she had engaged in at least one useful thing while she was here. As soon as the ladies who went on the hike disappeared down the trail, she and a few of her co-conspirators started covering the bottom of all the windows in the dining room with some old newspapers one of them had found in a storeroom. The result wasn't attractive, but it served the purpose of making them feel a bit more secure in these woods. For the most part, the women in attendance were city dwellers and they were uncomfortable with the isolation of their surroundings.

The talk last night about horror movies and zombies had frightened many of them. They knew that these things were all figments of the imagination, but they were also aware that real live people could be more of a horror show than the make-believe versions.

After the deed was done, the brief moment of camaraderie disappeared when each woman retreated to her room. Miss Fanny was grateful to have the room to herself. Autumn and Viola were on the hike, and that blasted Lucretia was in the kitchen fixing lunch with some of the ladies. Miss Fanny was supposed to be in there with them, but begged off feigning a headache. She hadn't lied.

Being around some of these old crows did make her head hurt.

Since there was no television, radio, or absolutely anything else to do, Miss Fanny opened the paperback she had brought with her to read. She was doing just that when the sound of clamoring feet and loud voices caught her attention. Slipping her shoes on she hurried down the hall to the front entrance where the hikers were filing into the building. They looked upset.

"Shut that door and lock it!" Bea directed. "Everybody to the dining room!"

Miss Fanny was bewildered. "What's going on?"

"Murder!" Thelma gasped as she hurriedly followed the others.

Miss Fanny's jaw dropped. She turned to Lucretia who had drifted into the foyer. She looked as befuddled as Miss Fanny.

"Did she say murder?"

Miss Fanny nodded. "That's what she said!"

The two of them followed the others. As expected, the dining room was in chaos. The fear was palpable.

"Hattie, check the door in the kitchen to make sure it's locked," Bea ordered. She then told the gathering about finding George Hadley's body. The women reacted with shock, tears and alarm.

"But that's only the tip of the iceberg!" Ethel Pramby's tone was rife with resentment. "While we were on our way back here, we told Dorothy and Thelma to use their cell phones to call the police. And you'll never guess what they told us. Tell them, ladies! Go ahead, tell them!"

Accusing eyes turned toward the two group leaders. Stepping forward, Dorothy cleared her throat.

"I'm sorry to say that Thelma mistakenly left her cell phone back at the church and I forgot my charger. My cell phone is dead."

The uproar was immediate.

"You mean we're stuck out here and can't talk to anybody on the outside?"

"A killer is stalking the woods and we can't get help?"

"What kind of trip planners are you?"

The insults and accusations were scathing. Neither woman tried to defend herself. Tired of the uproar, Connie stood up, took her shoe off and started banging it on the table until the noise died down.

"Okay, everybody's had their say. A mistake was made. Get over it because we have to focus."

A defiant Lucretia stood and challenged Connie. "And who are you to give us orders?"

Connie patted her pocket. "I'm the woman with a gun. Now, *sit down*."

Lucretia took a seat.

"Any other questions?" asked Hattie. Silence reigned.

Bea continued. "Now, since that's settled. We can get down to business. Are there any suggestions about how we can contact the outside?"

"That caretaker is coming back today to check on us, right?" Ruth Rivers asked.

"He said today or tomorrow," Thelma answered, relieved to offer some hope. She felt badly about the cell phone.

"He might not come today and tomorrow might be too late," Ethel offered. "We could all be dead by then."

"Thanks for those words of encouragement, Ethel," Bea cracked. "Does anybody have a *helpful* suggestion?"

"Why don't I drive the bus to the nearest town and go get help?" Dorothy felt equally as bad about the phones. She wanted to make amends.

Bea looked thoughtful. "That might not be a bad idea."

"Oh really?" Viola didn't seem so sure. "I know Dorothy drove a school bus, but can she handle a big bus like that?"

Dorothy gave Viola a look that could kill. "You've *got* to be kidding."

"I'm sure she could handle it, as a matter of fact I noticed that the keys were still in the ignition," said Bea. "The only problem is the body is aboard the bus and I'm not sure the bus should be moved. There might be evidence inside of it and outside too."

"We can mark the spot where it's parked," Thelma suggested.

"Good idea," Bea agreed.

"And believe me, nobody is going to touch that body," Hattie piped in.

"Who wants to get on the bus with a dead body?" Angela Rivers shivered at the thought.

"Well if I'm going to drive it, I don't have a choice do I?" Dorothy asked

"The body can be covered," Miss Fanny suggested. "We found a tarp when some of us were rattling around in the store room."

"That's a good idea too." Bea looked up at the covered windows. "And some of us want to thank you for your quick thinking, considering it was done before you knew what had happened. At least whoever might be lurking outside can't see inside here."

"Do you really think somebody might be out there?" an attendee asked.

"Who knows?" another one answered.

"Be sure to draw the curtains in your rooms," Thelma told the ladies. "Did somebody draw the blinds in the foyer?"

"I did," someone hollered from the crowd.

"Okay, so Dorothy will drive the bus to that town we passed a few miles back to get some help. Raise your hands if you agree."

All hands went up. It was the first time since they arrived at the retreat that there was a consensus.

"She's not going alone is she?" a voice from the group asked.

"Who's going with her?" Miss Fanny wanted to know.

The question was met with silence. Finally, Thelma took a deep breath.

"I'll go with her." She wasn't thrilled about the prospect, but she did help plan the trip and Dorothy *was* her best friend.

"I'll go too," Bea volunteered. "After all I'm the only licensed professional investigator here. The authorities might need my expertise."

"What expertise?" Ethel sneered.

Hattie came to Bea's defense. "I'll have you know that she has a certified license as a private investigator for the state of Indiana."

The skepticism was rampant and vocal. Bea ignored the doubters. She had the proof, even if it was tucked away in her purse which happened to be stashed in her room at the present. But, that was beside the point. Right now there was a crime to solve.

"Okay, so Dorothy, Thelma and me will be going…"

"I'll go too," Hattie interrupted.

"So I assume, Connie, that you're not going," Miss Fanny said hopefully. She knew how the three musketeers stuck together. "We need you here for security."

"That's logical," Bea concluded, "but we will need Connie to walk us through the woods to the bus, just in case. Then we'll need some volunteers to walk back to the center with her."

Autumn, Rosemary and Gladys volunteered for that duty as the spirit of cooperation filtered throughout the room. Bea was pleased.

"All right, then that's settled."

The meeting was adjourned and the group of volunteers prepared to make their way back to the bus. Bea whispered to Dorothy.

"Are there any more sharp knives left in the kitchen? I need one."

Unzipping the backpack she planned on taking with her, Dorothy withdrew a nice size blade. "You can have this." She patted her jacket pocket. "I have another one."

CHAPTER 9

The chosen contingent followed the road where the vehicle was discovered. With gun ready and knives drawn they formed a tight cluster. All eyes and ears were alert for anything unusual as they moved forward.

Limbs that only an hour ago had been moving stiffly along hiking trails were now moving with the flexibility of marathon trainees. Survival was the objective. No one wasted breath on chit chat, everyone was too busy watching for anything that moved. A murderer was stalking them and no one knew who the next victim would be.

When they reached the bus the ladies approached it with caution. Bea, Hattie and Connie looked at each other apprehensively. This was the real thing. No more theories, no more conjectures, a human life had actually been taken.

Dorothy stepped toward the bus door that had been left ajar. She hesitated.

"I've never seen a dead body that's not in a casket," she informed her companions.

"Me either," the others admitted. Nobody was looking forward to stepping onto the bus.

"We'll put this over his body." Bea indicated the tarp that she was carrying.

"*We* who?" Hattie wanted to know.

Dorothy shook her head. "I'm driving the bus with a dead body inside it. I want it covered before I go in there."

Bea turned her attention to Thelma. "What about you?"

Thelma offered no excuses. "No thanks."

Autumn stepped forward. "Give me the tarp. I'll do it."

She took the cover from Bea, opened the bus door and lead the way inside. Bea followed.

The interior was eerily quiet. It reminded Bea of a tomb.

"You take one end, I'll take the other," Autumn directed.

Together Bea and Autumn unfolded the tarp. Looking away from the body, the younger woman stepped over it as Bea forced herself to memorize every detail of the grisly scene. She hoped against hope that she would never see such a sight again.

"I didn't notice it before but that butcher knife looks like the ones that were in the kitchen drawer at the conference center…"

"Before all the women stole them," Autumn said dryly.

"And it's driven into him all the way to the handle." Bea shivered slightly at the realization. "It took a lot of force to do something like that."

"And a lot of anger," Autumn quietly observed.

They placed the cover over the remains of the late George Hadley.

"Rest in Peace," Bea whispered.

"We should say a prayer for him."

Bea and Autumn jumped, startled by the unexpected voice. They looked up to see Hattie boarding the bus, followed by Connie, while Dorothy stood on the steps peering over the railing.

"The body is covered," Hattie called back to the others before coming fully aboard. Thelma, Rosemary and Gladys remained crowded together on the steps. Everyone on board avoided getting too close to the covered corpse.

"Is he stiff yet?' Gladys inquired.

Bea shot her an annoyed look. "I don't know. Why don't you touch him and see for yourself."

"I just asked," Gladys said defensively, looking away guiltily.

Bea turned to Hattie. "Would you lead us in prayer?"

The ladies closed their eyes and bowed their heads. Hattie looked skyward.

"Lord! We're here to send the soul of the dearly departed Mr. John …"

"George," Dorothy whispered.

"George Headley…"

"Hadley," Thelma corrected.

"Hadley, and we hope that you accept him in your name. We don't know much about him, only you know the good and the bad. But we pray that you'll accept him into your kingdom so that he might sit at your feet and bask in your glory.

"And while you're at it Lord, please shower your goodness and mercy on us your *living* servants stuck out here in these woods. We trust that you will guide this bus to safety so that we can get back to our families..."

"Amen!" Gladys interjected loudly. Her spirited encouragement served to fuel Hattie's religious fervor.

"Deliver us from evil, Lord! Protect us from danger! Yea, tho we walk through the valley of the shadow of death, we will fear no evil. Thy rod and thy staff they comfort us…"

Connie opened one eye to find Bea also peeking at Hattie. They knew their friend well. She was working herself into a marathon prayer session, and they didn't have the time. Bea gave Connie a silent signal as Hattie continued.

"Thy prepareth,…"

"A rescue mission for us to go on, Lord, and we're grateful," Bea finished.

"Amen," Connie proclaimed.

"Thank you, Hattie," Dorothy said quickly. She was also familiar with Hattie's long winded prayers. "We better get going."

Settling into the driver's seat, she fingered the keys hanging in the ignition. The ladies who were returning to the conference center scampered off the bus. Thelma made a move to join them.

"You're supposed to be going with us." Bea reminded her. She took a seat behind Dorothy.

"Thelma and me was talking before we came on board and decided that it's best for one of the conference planners to stay at the center," Dorothy explained. "Lord knows what will happen with those battling biddies if all the leaders are gone."

Thelma nodded. "Somebody has to be in charge."

"Good thinking." Hattie agreed, taking a seat across the aisle from Bea.

Exiting the bus behind Thelma and Autumn, Connie waved goodbye. "Be safe and hurry back."

Dorothy closed the doors, turned the key and pressed the accelerator. The engine sputtered. She tried again. It started. She shifted gears.

The other women waved goodbye as the big bus rolled away, watching as it slowly picked up speed and traveled down the road.

Connie released the safety on her weapon, placed the gun in her pocket and turned in the opposite direction. "Okay, ladies. Let's go."

****

Miss Fanny was so tired of Lucretia Martin she didn't know what to do. On top of being a big mouth the woman was a worry wart. She had everybody in the building upset with her comments about how late it was getting and how the other women weren't back yet.

"What are we going to do if something happens to them?" Lucretia asked anybody who would listen. "We need a plan."

Fanny had reminded her that so far the lower windows in the dining room were covered, as were the other windows that didn't have blinds or curtains. Chairs had been stacked against all exit doors and every woman in the building who could find a knife was armed with one.

"What else do you want us to do?" Miss Fanny asked impatiently as she tried to relax in the bedroom she shared with her worrisome roommate.

"I don't know," Lucretia whined. "But we've got to think of something."

"Well, it's about time for our church members to start dinner. You can go in the kitchen and help until you come up with something," Miss Fanny suggested, hoping that she would get the hint.

Since she didn't budge, Miss Fanny came up with a unique idea to get her out of the room. Miss Fanny suggested a way Lucretia and the other ladies might be able to defend themselves. It wasn't until Connie shook her awake from a nap that Miss Fanny discovered how effective her suggestion to Lucretia had been.

Miss Fanny sat up in bed and welcomed her back. "Glad to see you. Did the others get off okay?"

"Yes, it shouldn't be long before they bring back some help." Connie settled on the end of the bed at the older woman's feet. "Instead of going with them, Thelma came back with us to try and keep the peace around here. From the looks of it, I'm glad she did."

Miss Fanny sat on the edge of her bed. "Oh yeah? What's going on?"

Connie frowned. "You tell me. From what I heard it was your idea."

"What are you talking about?"

"Put your shoes on and follow me."

Miss Fanny complied and walked down the hallway with Connie until they reached one of the rooms that served as a small meeting space. Muffled voices could be heard behind the closed door. Connie opened it.

There stood a dozen or more women, dressed in sweat suits and jeans. Posed in a defensive stance, each of them was holding a knife. At the front of the room stood their leader, Lucretia Martin, knife in hand.

"Okay, step and stab," she instructed the others. In unison, the women stepped forward and thrust their knives out and upward.

A tight-lipped Connie threw Miss Fanny an accusing glare. "Lucretia told me that this Step and Stab class was your idea."

"It sure was," Lucretia said brightly. "Fanny said she saw it on TV on some self defense program. She even showed me how to do it and suggested that I show the others."

Connie's eyes narrowed. "Really, Miss Fanny? Step and Stab?"

A non-repentant Miss Fanny shrugged. "Sounded good to me."

Frustrated, Connie turned back to Lucretia. "You don't know what you're doing. You'll fool around and get yourselves killed."

Lucretia disagreed. "No, you got that wrong. I'm teaching these ladies how *not* to get killed."

"I guess she told you." Miss Fanny gave a satisfied grin.

With nothing more to say, Connie closed the door as the Step and Stab class resumed. Silently, she whispered an urgent prayer that her friends would get back *very* soon.

****

"What do you mean, something's wrong with the bus?" Bea peered over the seat at Dorothy questioningly.

"I don't hear anything," Hattie added, responding to Dorothy's insistence that she heard a sound coming from under the hood.

"I'm telling you, I've been driving buses for too many years not to recognize when something doesn't sound right. I'm pulling over."

Bea looked alarm. "For what?"

"It's dark out here!" Hattie looked out the window warily. "Maybe we can drive along until we reach the highway. I'd rather stop there than here."

"Looks like we're not going to make the highway," Dorothy warned as the bus began to slow down.

She pumped the accelerator to no avail. All three women watched with growing dismay as the bus' speed gradually diminished until it came to a complete stop. No one made a sound.

Turning the key off, Dorothy waited a few seconds and then turned the key back to start. The engine sputtered.

She repeated her actions. It sputtered again, but the engine only emitted a faint whir. Dorothy tried once more. This time, nothing and all the lights on the bus went off plunging them into complete darkness.

"You have got to be kidding!" Dorothy shrieked.

"Try one more time," Bea urged.

Dorothy sighed. "It won't make a difference. The lights are off. That means the battery is dead."

"Oh, Lord!" Hattie moaned. "What are we going to do?"

"Walk back to the center." Dorothy grabbed the flashlight she had brought with her and swung out of the driver's seat. "What else can we do?'

Left unsaid was the fear each of them harbored about taking the journey through the woods where a killer might be loose.

"At least we have flashlights," Bea said, trying to reassure herself that everything would be fine."

"I don't," Hattie reminded them. She gave herself a mental kick for having forgotten such an essential item.

"There should be another one around here." Using her flashlight, Dorothy began searching the driver's area, around the seat, the sun visor and the dash board. "The man's a bus driver. There are certain things he should have with him—a flashlight, map, a GPS or something. Plus he's a long distance bus driver. He's got to be carrying some sort of bag. Anything he needs might be in there." Dorothy looked in the space behind the driver's seat where she used to stash her own bag. Nothing.

"Come on, Dorothy, take your flashlight and let's search the luggage carriers."

Hattie watched wide-eyed, praying that a third flashlight would be found. The more light they had traipsing through these woods the better, but again they found nothing. Returning to the front of the bus, Bea looked thoughtful.

"Hmmmm, this is curious," Bea pondered aloud. "A busted radio receiver, no traveling bag…" She turned and approached the covered corpse.

"What are you doing?" Hattie asked.

"I'm going to see if Mr. Hadley has a cell phone on him."

"Yeah," Dorothy said eagerly. "He had to have some sort of communication if the radio didn't work. Shoot, Bea, you might turn out to be a pretty good investigator after all."

"Gee, thanks." Bea said sarcastically. "I wish I had thought of it earlier. But, better late than never."

"You're going to touch a dead body?" Hattie was horrified.

Bea leveled her with a look. "You're in the funeral planning business. You work with dead people all the time."

"I work with their survivors. Except for my Leon, I ain't never touched another dead person."

Taking a moment to calm herself, Bea moved forward. Gingerly pulling back the tarp, she bent and quickly patted the man's pockets. Finding nothing, she replaced the cover.

"I guess that's that." She sighed in frustration. "If he had a bag, the cell phone was probably in there."

They could procrastinate no longer. Reluctantly, the women stepped off the bus. For a few seconds they stood listening to every sound around them. Nobody was looking forward to the trip back.

"Now we have even further to walk." Hattie groaned, reminding the others how far they had driven before the bus stopped. "I hope he's not out there waiting."

"He better not be." Checking her fanny pack, Dorothy made sure the kitchen knife she was carrying was handy. "I've got something for him."

Withdrawing her own weapon, Bea stood with a knife in one hand and a flashlight in the other. "Is everybody ready?"

Hattie and Dorothy nodded. The three of them started walking down the blacktop road, guided by the beams from their flashlights. The farther they walked, the less distance they seemed to be gaining.

"Talk about bad luck," said Bea. "Lord knows how far we've got to go."

Dorothy agreed. "I don't think things can get much worse."

The words had hardly left her mouth when the sound of thunder rumbled ominously in the distance. A flash of lightening lit up the darkened sky.

Even Hattie contributed to the unanimous response to Mother Nature's warning.

"Oh, shit!"

CHAPTER 10

Connie sat in an over-stuffed chair on the periphery of the dining room thumbing through a magazine. From outward appearances she seemed perfectly relaxed, but her mind was on her friends on the bus. It was raining. The downpour beat steadily against the windowpanes. A rumble of thunder followed by a streak of lightening added to her uneasiness about their journey. Night had fallen and the rescue party had been gone much longer than anyone anticipated. She was worried. Silently, she whispered a prayer for their safe journey with the hope that they would soon bring help back to all of them.

Looking up, she observed clusters of women discussing the day's events. Another topic of conversation was Lucretia's Step and Stab class, which appeared to have boosted the morale of some of her "students."

"I'm going to kick some killer butt if he tries to get in here," one of them boasted to the others with confidence.

Thelma wandered over to Connie. "Is it me or have you noticed something different about our ladies."

Connie's eyes took in the room full of women. "You mean the fact that there's a lot more laughing and talking going on now?"

"Exactly. I think we're making some progress."

Connie chuckled. "I guess it's easier to be friends when a mad killer might be lurking outside."

"Amen to that."

Thelma's stomach gave a rumbling growl loud enough for the women sitting nearby to hear. The group burst into laughter.

"Sounds like somebody's hungry," one of them teased.

"You're right about that," Thelma answered good-naturedly.

"I'm with you," Connie declared. "There's got to be enough leftovers from dinner to make sandwiches."

She, Thelma and a couple of other women made a noisy retreat into the kitchen. Miss Fanny shook her head in amusement.

"Mark my words, on Judgment Day when the Lord calls Connie's name, she'll have a mouth full of food and won't be able to answer. That woman sure likes to eat."

"Leave her alone, there's nothing wrong with that," admonished Viola Smith from nearby.

Lucretia raised a surprised brow. Both she and Viola had been wary of Connie Palmer. Neither one of them quite knew what to think of her.

"When did you become a fan of Connie's?" she wanted to know.

"When she found out Connie carries a gun." Miss Fanny quipped, defying her to dispute the fact.

"We're out here in the middle of nowhere, being stalked by a madman, and she's got the only weapon that matters. I'm not about to antagonize her," Viola declared.

"Antagonize who?" Carrying a well endowed sandwich, the lady in question entered the dining room and wandered over to where they were sitting.

"What have you got there?" asked Miss Fanny as Connie sat down across from her.

"Thick slices of ham, sitting on a bed of lettuce with pickles and tomatoes, all lying between two slices of wheat bread." Connie took a bite and moaned with pleasure.

"I rest my case." Miss Fanny said in triumph. "Connie, I was telling the others how you sure like to eat."

"No lie, if God didn't intend for us to eat, he wouldn't have created food." Connie took another bite of her sandwich, while the ladies laughed at her unusual observation. "Now who's being antagonized?" Connie repeated.

"We were talking about Viola and how she wants to kiss your tail because you have a gun." Miss Fanny gave Connie a roguish grin. "Suddenly, she's your biggest fan."

Viola quickly spoke up. "I only pointed out that if we're being stalked, we have something better than knives to protect ourselves."

"Why would the killer stalk us?" asked one of the women overhearing the comment.

"Maybe he thinks we have money," another one offered.

Lucretia spoke up. "I don't know why. Most of us are on Social Security and pensions."

"But he wouldn't know that," someone observed.

Ruth Rivers, one of Connie's roommates chimed in, "That's true. We're a nice looking group, but we don't exactly scream 'wealthy.' Besides, if whoever is out there was looking to rob us, why kill Mr. Hadley?"

"That's easy." Lucretia smirked. "Because the murderer is one of those maniac serial killers and right now, he's got us right where he wants us." Her eyes moved around the room slowly until she was satisfied that she was the center of attention. "Don't you see? Now he can come back and pick us off *one* by *one*."

"Just like in *Friday the Thirteenth*, and *Scream*," Ruth's daughter, Angela added.

Viola nodded grimly. "That's what I'm saying."

"Don't start talking about that scary movie mess," Ruth warned.

Miss Fanny had had enough. "Ya'll got to be crazy! The Good Book might say 'blessed are the peacemakers', but nowhere in there does it say, blessed are the stupid. If you think I would just let somebody break in and kill me without putting up a fight, none of you have the sense that God gave a goose. Whoever's out there, if he tries to come in *here* he's a dead man."

There was a loud chorus of agreement.

Autumn, who had been sitting by herself in a corner of the room, approached the rest of the ladies. "But, is it right to *anticipate* killing someone? Here we are Christian women at a reconciliation retreat and we're in here talking about Connie's gun and taking step and stab classes like we're relishing the idea of hurting somebody, not dreading it. Taking a person's life is serious."

"She's got a point," Angela conceded, but Viola bristled, turning on Autumn.

"Well ain't you little goody two-shoes. You're telling us that it's wrong to want to protect ourselves?" She turned to Connie. "If the murderer tries to get in here, tell Autumn what you *anticipate* doing with that gun?"

Connie didn't hesitate. "Shoot first and ask questions later. But let's hope it won't come to that."

"Let's hope not," Autumn sighed.

"Before we get all out of kilter about this," Lucretia grumbled, "if somebody does get in here to harm us, nothing will probably happen anyway. I'll bet you dollars to donuts that Connie's never even fired that gun, let alone shot anyone." She looked at the subject of her comment skeptically.

The spotlight was on Connie. She cleared her throat and answered softly.

"Actually, I've done both."

An audible gasp swept the room.

"Now look here, Lucretia, you done opened your big mouth once too often. Somebody's gonna bust you in it one of these days." Miss Fanny looked as though she would be the one to do it.

Connie held up her hand to stay further words from her supporter.

"It's okay. I'll take care of this." She turned to Lucretia. "For your information, I wasn't raised to be a submissive, sweet, helpless woman. I'm not afraid to take care of business and defend myself. When anything threatens me or someone I care about, I deal with it head on."

"Oooh, weeee! I guess she told you," one of the women said, laughing raucously.

Lucretia was mortified. "Well, I didn't mean anything by what I said."

Connie accepted her apology with a dismissive wave of her hand, but Viola's eyes narrowed with resentment as she glared at Autumn.

"It was her that started this, with all that *anticipation* mess."

Looking undisturbed by the comment, Autumn was about to address Viola when one of the members of CLUCK Baptist appeared in the dining room stopping all conversation. The woman looked terrified.

"Somebody's trying to get in the front door," she croaked frantically.

Everyone in the room rushed to the foyer. There they found Pearl Mason huddled by the door. As the women advanced, she put a finger to her lips to quiet them and then pointed to the barricaded, beveled glass door. A flash of lightning illuminated the outline of someone standing outside. The door handle turned.

"It's the killer!" A woman whimpered.

There was another clap of thunder. The handle turned again, followed by a frenzied knock.

"Quiet!" Connie warned the women as she pulled her gun from her pocket. "Can you hear that?"

Everyone strained to listen. Faint voices could be heard on the other side of the door. There was another flurry of knocks.

"Hey, in there!"

"Open up, it's us."

"Hurry up before we get electrocuted!"

"That's Hattie" said Miss Fanny. "I'd know that voice anywhere." She hollered out. "Hattie, is that you out there!"

A muffled voice answered. "Yes it is! Let us in before we drown."

One of the women called out to them. "Is the killer with you?"

"Let us in or I'll kill *you*!" Bea screamed.

A few of the ladies rushed to remove the chairs stacked against the front door.

"It could be a trick," Lucretia warned. "Get your knives ready."

The ladies tensed as the lock was released. The door was opened a crack and Thelma peeked outside.

"It's them."

She stood back as the shivering, rain soaked rescuers filed inside. Cheers of relief filled the air.

"We're saved."

"Did you bring the police?

"Thank you, Jesus!"

A disheveled Dorothy shouted over the crowd. "Oh, shut up! No, we don't have the police with us. We didn't even get out of the woods."

Thelma looked stunned. "What do you mean? Did you get lost?"

"The bus died on us." Bea swiped at the water trickling down her face.

"We had to walk back." Hattie emitted a sneeze.

The disappointed groans drowned her out. Bea waved them to silence.

"*But* we're no worse off than before. We'll just wait until morning to see if Mr. Lucas comes to see about us."

Viola mumbled, "Let's pray it's not too late."

CHAPTER 11

Miss Fanny's eyes narrowed as she looked across the room at Viola Smith. She and her roommates were supposed to be relaxing, but Viola had been talking nonstop. *That blasted woman thought she was an authority on everything.*

"I knew that Hattie, Bea and Dorothy taking that bus to Lord-knows-where was a bad idea in the first place," Viola told the others. "I figured the murderer did something to the bus. As for the rain, I knew it was coming. I could smell it."

"From inside the building?" Miss Fanny retorted.

"My nose is very sensitive." Viola sniffed as though to confirm her declaration. "As the reigning first lady of Twelve Disciples I have to be attuned to everything around me."

"That is so true," Lucretia Martin said haughtily "I recall *that* being a requirement when *I* was first lady of Mt. Malachi. Service to others was *my* main goal."

"So true, so true," Viola agreed.

"*But*, times have changed. Haven't they Autumn?" Lucretia's catty tone made it clear that the younger woman was an unwanted part of that change.

"It must have if you can smell water through brick walls," Autumn cracked, never taking her eyes from the novel she was reading.

Miss Fanny cackled with delight. She liked this woman! Although Autumn was the subject of a lot of negativity, she held her own against vipers such as the ones she now faced.

Viola raised a disapproving brow. "You know, Autumn, I've noticed something that's disturbing. You can be very disrespectful when you want to be."

Autumn raised her eyes from her book. The look she gave Viola spoke volumes. "My mother taught me to respect anyone who respects me, and to *beware* of people who don't."

Lucretia piped in. "Wouldn't your mother be around your husband's age?"

"Yes, ma'am, and my *great* grandmother is around your age." Autumn resumed reading.

Lucretia looked confused. She wasn't sure whether she had been insulted or not. Viola didn't have similar reservations. She was about to respond when Fanny intervened.

"There's going to be two more murders around here if I have to hear another word from either of you." She leveled Viola and Lucretia with a warning look.

As the women sputtered and stuttered in response, Autumn tossed her book aside and got up from her bed.

"I'm going to the evening workshop. I believe it's titled *Can We All Get Along?* It's good to know that despite everything that's happened, *somebody* still remembers the purpose of this trip." She left the room.

"Wait up," Miss Fanny called after her. "I'm getting out of here too." She wasn't about to stay in the room with those two snakes. Let them poison one another.

Walking down the hallway Miss Fanny passed the room occupied by Hattie and Bea. Connie was seated in a chair near the door visiting. Miss Fanny stuck her head inside.

"Are you ladies going to the workshop?"

They responded in the negative, informing her that Hattie was already there. Miss Fanny and Autumn continued on their way.

Bea was sipping a cup of tea as she complained to Connie. "Shoot, I'm chilled to the bone. The last thing I want to do is spend another second in a workshop with some of the nuts in this place. I'm already stuck in this room with two dingbats. Laverne sounds like a hyena when she laughs and Rosemary is some kind of neat freak."

"I heard from one of your church members that Laverne was obsessive compulsive," Connie related to Bea.

"A fancy word for mental case," Bea concluded. "You should have seen her before she left the room. She spent nearly twenty minutes smoothing wrinkles out of her bedspread. What's going on in your room?"

"Well, Mrs. Rivers and her daughter have decided that I'm going to hell and need saving. So they've been holding prayer sessions in our room for the killer's soul and throwing my name in for good measure."

Bea howled with laughter. For years Hattie had been declaring that the free spirited Connie was bound for hell. One of her missions in life was trying to save her friend from eternal flames. "It looks like Hattie's getting some help."

"Oh, that's not the worst of it," Connie continued. "You know Pearl Mason fancies herself as being a singer."

"Ha!" Bea scoffed.

"I agree, but it seems that she's also on this crusade to do some soul saving. Before she went to the workshop, she broke into some sort of rendition of *Precious Lord*. At least I think that was what she was trying to sing. The song was so off key I really couldn't recognize it."

"That's Pearl, whenever the spirit hits her she breaks into song."

Connie was less subtle. "All I know is that I'd rather go out in this thunder storm, in the dark, with a murderer stalking me then have to hear her again."

"And I'll go with you." Bea finished her tea. "I don't know how Hattie puts up with these folks. I've got to give her credit, despite everything that's happened she's still trying to keep this thing together. She came rushing in here, dried off, changed her clothes and then went to the meeting room. I hope she doesn't catch pneumonia."

"She gets an E for effort."

Just then Miss Fanny stalked into the room. She didn't look happy.

"Ya'll, get to the conference room. Hattie needs some support, because all hell is about to break loose. That big mouth Viola and that ignorant heifer, Lucretia, came down to the workshop stirring up some mess. I'm about two seconds from kicking both their behinds. Hattie is *my* daughter-in-law, ain't nobody gonna abuse her but me and her friends. Come on!"

Bea scrambled out of the bed and Connie rose from the chair. Both of them were bone weary, but Hattie needed their help.

"Let's go," they said in unison. Like avenging angels the three women charged to the rescue.

****

"Can't we all get along my foot!" Lucretia was shouting at Hattie when Miss Fanny and her reinforcements entered. Hattie stood at the podium trying in vain to address the gathering.

"Ladies…Ladies…"

Viola was vehement. "Since your disastrous attempt to get help ended in failure, we're now trapped here like animals and we're easy targets."

"No, we're not!" Thelma was standing beside Hattie making an effort to keep everyone calm. "We're women of faith, here for a purpose…"

"Forget that! We want outta here!" Viola yelled. "It's thundering and lightening outside…"

"Which is God's work at its best," Hattie assured everyone.

"We know that," said Lucretia. "What we don't know is how and when we're getting out of here."

"Oh ye of little faith," someone said from the back of the room.

Heads swiveled in the voice's direction. It was Autumn Randall speaking.

"You know what? I wasn't thrilled about coming on this retreat. I let my husband talk me into it. He said that it might be good for me to spend time with women of faith outside our church to try and heal the wounds between us. Personally, I was skeptical, and it looks like I was right. Since getting on the bus, all I've found is a lot of sniping and gripping, but no healing, and *definitely* no faith."

For a split second her words silenced the room. Miss Fanny took that opportunity to speak up.

"Why is it that this woman seems to be the only voice of reason around here? We older women should be examples for the younger ones, not vice versa. It's no wonder young people don't want to go to church these days…"

"Or some older ones either," Connie added. "I know I don't want to be surrounded by negative people like the ones I've met here at this retreat. Looks like the only time we can get along is when we think we're in danger."

"So, I guess the message I'm taking back with me is that death unites, and life divides," Autumn concluded.

Once again her words were met with shamed silence by most in attendance, and looks of resentment from Viola and Lucretia. Suddenly, Pearl Mason, rose from her chair, closed her eyes, threw her head back and began singing loudly: *"Lord don't move that mountain, but give me the strength to climb…"*

Eyes widened. Mouths dropped open. To their credit, no one covered their ears, but Connie, Bea and Miss Fanny shortened their rescue mission as they made a hasty retreat.

CHAPTER 12

Outside the conference center, the increasing intensity of the torrential downpour was impossible to ignore. So was the discord inside.

After Pearl's impromptu concert, instead of reconciling, the ladies attending the workshop began to huddle in small clusters with fellow church members. Led by the acrimony between Viola, Lucretia and Autumn, it was now Twelve Disciples and Mount Malachi versus CLUCK Baptist.

"Satan is busy today," Hattie observed as she and Dorothy stood on the side watching the ladies.

"For a while it seemed everyone was coming together," Dorothy said sadly. "But it looks like things are falling apart again and Lord knows, Pearl's howling like a prairie dog didn't help."

"No lie," Hattie admitted mournfully. "Maybe this conference wasn't such a good idea."

"Ya think?" Dorothy's words oozed sarcasm. Hattie's hurt expression didn't stem her bitter recriminations. "Me and Thelma tried to tell you this was a bad idea, but *no*, Hattie Collier was going to throw the Good Book at 'em and make things right with the world."

"Now, Dorothy, you know that bad blood between churches is *not* the Lord's way. We had to do something."

"We did it all right." Dorothy waved her hands toward the room. "From the look of it they're going to kill each other before the stalker does the job."

Hattie was indignant. "Don't you dare blame this on me! It's Viola and Lucretia starting this trouble. I still think this retreat was the right thing to do."

"I don't blame you. I blame Thelma and me for being dumb enough to listen to you. After this we'll be lucky if anyone ever signs up with the Road Wanderers again!"

With that parting shot, Dorothy stalked past Bea and Connie as they were re-entering the room. The end of Pearl's unwelcomed concert brought them back to see about Hattie.

"What was that about?" Bea's questioning look followed Dorothy.

"She's trying to blame this rotten trip on me," Hattie whined.

Rotten trip? Bea and Connie's eyes met in agreement, but they remained silent.

A loud rumble of thunder was followed by a brilliant flash of lightening. All the women in the room froze. The lights flickered just as Miss Fanny ambled back into the room.

"Something tells me we'd better gather all the flashlights and candles we can find before the lights go out," Miss Fanny cautioned.

The words were barely out of her mouth when most of the feuding ladies rushed out of the room in search of candles and flashlights. Miss Fanny winked at Hattie.

"Nothing says togetherness like fear of being in the dark."

Twenty minutes later, all of the ladies were assembled in the dining room depositing their findings—five flashlights and fifteen candles.

"Let the lights go out. We're ready for any emergency now," Angela Rivers declared.

"Don't go wishing for something we don't want." Lucretia warned.

"The only question now is does anyone have any matches?" As far as Bea was concerned, this gathering was in serious need of some survival training. Her observation was verified when not one person could come up with a single match.

"What are we going to do if the lights go out?" Angela wailed.

"We've got the flashlights," her mother, Ruth, reassured her.

Angela wasn't convinced. "But how about extra batteries? We don't have any of those?"

"We'll be fine," Dorothy sought to sooth everyone's fears.

Autumn raised her hand to get the ladies' attention. "I think I can solve the match problem. I saw some around. I'll go see if they're still there." She left the room.

"Superwoman to the rescue," Viola whispered loud enough for those around her to hear.

"As always," Lucretia replied, stifling a yawn. "It's getting late. I'm tired. Is anybody else in here ready for bed?"

"Not with thunder storms, murderers and Lord knows what else going on around here," Angela declared. "I'm staying up until daylight when I can see outside." Many of the other women agreed.

"You're a young woman and can afford to lose sleep," Lucretia told her. "I can't."

Lucretia was sitting in a chair near the covered windows and was pulling herself up to leave when she halted in her effort. Nobody noticed.

Returning to the dining room, Autumn went to the table where the candles and flash lights had been placed. She added a pack of matches. Angela thanked her profusely.

By now the group's chatter had diminished. The ladies were lethargic, too exhausted and uneasy to engage in conversation as the storm raged outside. The room was eerily silent, but not for long.

"Did you hear that?" Lucretia got to her feet. Her face was drawn. She looked apprehensive. Everyone turned to look at her.

"Hear what?" Hattie asked. "If you mean the storm, of course we heard it."

"No. There's something outside. I *heard* it." There was certainty in her fear-laced voice.

Murmurs of concern drifted through the room.

"What did you hear?" Bea inquired, listening closely.

"Pecking."

"Pecking?"

Lucretia nodded. "I hear something pecking on one of the windows."

"I don't hear anything. It must have been a bird," Bea suggested.

"Maybe it's a branch from a tree," Connie offered.

"There's no reason a bird would be pecking..." Lucretia's sentence was cut short as a loud yelp came from across the room.

"What?" Several startled women turned in the direction of the disturbance.

Angela, who had been checking the covered windows to make sure the papers were secure, was now backing away from them as though they had come to life.

"Something *is* tapping on the window," she announced in a stage whisper.

"I told you so," Lucretia sneered.

"I heard it too!" Viola declared.

"Look!" Pearl Mason pointed a shaky finger at a window near the large fireplace. There was no denying the circle of light coming from the outside. It danced up and down the window and then back and forth across it.

"It looks like a flashlight," one of the ladies observed.

Ruth Rivers pointed to an identical circle of light playing across another window. "Look at that!"

"The murderer! He found us!" Angela croaked.

"There might be more than one of them." Viola stifled a scream. Fearful murmurs filled the rooms.

"Quiet!" Connie commanded. "Whoever is out there knows someone is in here, but they may not know how many we are."

Rosemary Sanders, from CLUCK Baptist, sprinted into the dining room. "Somebody's knocking on the front door."

Fear turned to terror. The situation was rapidly becoming chaotic.

"Go see who it is," she told Rosemary calmly.

The woman looked at her as if she had lost her mind. "Are you a fool? There's a murderer out there." Much to Bea's dismay, Rosemary burst into tears.

Amateurs! These women were really in need of a pro to lead them.

"Oh, stop blubbering," Bea ordered. "This is no time for panic. It might be the caregiver outside coming to see about us."

The room was abuzz with hope. Rosemary even perked up.

"The lights have disappeared," Angela informed them. "If it's him maybe he's going back to the front."

"And if it's not him, whoever it is might be dangerous and we have no one to depend on but ourselves," Bea warned.

"And the Lord," Hattie reminded them. She looked around at the gathering. "Repeat after me: no weapon formed against me shall prosper."

A few weak voices echoed her words. Hattie was adamant. "Say it! No weapon formed against me shall prosper."

This time the response was forceful. The women were galvanized. A muffled sound could be heard coming from the front of the building.

"It's that knocking again," Rosemary speculated. "He's back at the front door."

Lucretia called out. "Everyone in the step and stab class get ready."

Those who had their knives with them followed her directions. Others scattered to retrieve their weapons.

"Before we *stab* anybody, maybe some of us should go to the door and see who's there," Bea reasoned.

The ladies agreed. Miss Fanny began to bark orders.

"Some of ya'll take that step and stab mess to the back in case the front door is a decoy. Those who don't have knives, grab those chairs and that fireplace poker. Space out so you have room to fight. Connie, you've got the gun, you go to the door. Bea, you go with her."

Bea and Connie looked at each other in amazement. Miss Fanny had morphed into a general commanding her troops, and she was stealing Bea's thunder.

Borrowing a knife from one of the women, Bea turned to ask Connie, "Are you ready?"

Drawing her weapon, Connie released the safety. "Yep."

"I'm coming with you," said Hattie.

"Take this." Dorothy handed her one of her knives.

Leaving the dining room, the three of them inched their way down the hall to the front entranceway where the knocking became more insistent.

At the front door, Connie called out, "Who's there?"

A rumble of thunder nearly drowned out the reply, but the voice they heard was masculine.

"Let us in! We need shelter."

"Who are you?" Connie countered.

"Me and my buddies were camping and we got caught in the storm," was the reply.

"There's more than two of them," Hattie whispered frantically to Bea. Neither was pleased by that fact.

"Why didn't you knock first instead of trying to peek inside?" Bea wanted answers.

"Lady, we knocked before, but I guess you couldn't hear us," a second voice answered. "The wind's really whipping it up out here. There's a tornado headed this way! How about you let us in to sit this out?"

Tornado? The ladies looked at each other with uncertainty.

"That's the oldest trick in the book," Hattie declared.

The first voice called out again. "Haven't you checked your cell phones? You probably have an alert message from the weather bureau."

Knowing that they didn't have cell phones, Bea decided to bluff. "Go away or we'll call the police."

"Go ahead," voice number one yelled, "we've got no problem with that." The banging on the door resumed with even more force.

Pearl Mason came running to the foyer in a frenzy. "They're trying to break in the back door." That damn Viola opened the door and some man tried to push his way in."

Connie whirled in Pearl's direction. "What? Hattie and Bea stay here. I'll see what's going on." She rushed to the kitchen with Pearl on her heels.

The scene in the room was chaotic. A man was being crushed in the kitchen door. Only half of his body was visible. A group of women pushed against it frantically trying to keep him out. Between the grunts and cries of the woman and the man's screams of pain as some of the women stabbed at his body, the noise was deafening. After a quick assessment of the situation, Connie made a decision.

"Open the door," she ordered calmly.

"Are you crazy," said one of the defenders of the kitchen. "We're trying to keep him out."

"Open the damn door!" she commanded, gun in hand and ready to fire. There was no room for argument. The women stepped aside. The door opened.

Doubled over in pain and gasping for breath, the burly man stumbled into the room.

"You tried to kill me! You tried to stab me! You bitches must be crazy!" Any further words died in his throat as his eyes locked on the barrel of the gun pointed at him.

Connie's tone was deadly. "Step back. Go get your buddies and leave."

Gray eyes stared at her from under the bill of a baseball cap. "Now lady, be careful. Put that down before somebody gets hurt."

Connie didn't blink as she confronted the stranger. "I'm not going to repeat myself. Step out *now*."

The man took a step, but in the wrong direction. Her weapon gave a loud report. The women screamed and so did the man.

"Ow-w-w-! Mother..." The camper grabbed his ear. Blood trickled between his fingers. His eyes opened wide in shock. When he saw Connie's gun still pointed at him, he stumbled backward and out of the door. Connie quickly slammed, latched and bolted it. Mission accomplished.

CHAPTER 13

Viola tried her best to look innocent as the other women, angrily awaited her explanation for opening the door. Her eyes darted back and forth among them, but her contrition only lasted a second.

"It's not like I let him in on purpose," she declared. "I opened the door to check and see if the storm door was locked. It was so dark I didn't see him."

Connie was livid. "Viola, you *knew* those men were out there. They've been shining lights in the window, trying to find a vulnerable spot, and making up lies to get in. But you just opened the door!"

Viola was defiant. "Just for a split second and there he was!"

"Why did you open it at all?" Miss Fanny demanded. "Common sense should have told you not to do that."

"Look, Fanny, like I said, there was no way I could see him. Anyway, my intent was to try and protect us."

Connie would not be placated. "Didn't we say that the commotion up front might be a decoy for someone trying to get in back here?"

"Well I'm sorry, okay?" Viola shot back, completely on the defensive. "I messed up! What more can I say? Besides, Annie Oakley, you took care of everything with your big bad gun."

Squaring her shoulders, she made a move to leave the room. As far as she was concerned the matter was closed.

Connie was so mad that her voice was quivering. "Another mess up like that and Annie's *gonna* get her gun and you'll know what *sorry* is."

Viola challenged her. "Meaning what? You'll shoot me?"

As the two women were squaring off, Autumn rushed into the room. "Is everyone okay? What happened back here?" When no one responded she turned to Connie. "That was you shooting, right? What were you shooting at? We were scared to death that someone back here had been killed!"

"Girl, you should have seen it!" Pearl gushed. "Connie had us open the door for one of the killers and then she blasted him with her gun."

"What!" Autumn gasped.

Pearl elaborated. "She leaned back, as cool as a cucumber, and shot his ear off."

Autumn looked incredulous. The other women chuckled at Pearl's creative description. However, Connie was terse.

"That's not quite how it happened. I only grazed him, but never mind that, what's going on up front?"

"Bea wants you. Those two men outside are making a bigger ruckus than the storm."

"You mean those *three* men." Throwing Viola a pointed look, Connie stalked out of the room.

Confused, Autumn turned to the remaining women. "What's happening?"

"There are three men, not two," Miss Fanny explained. "One of them was back here and Viola opened the door and he nearly got in. If it hadn't been for Connie, we would have been goners."

"So, I'm the bad guy?" Viola groused.

"Yes!" chorused the other women.

Autumn shook her head in disbelief. "Well, as long as everything is under control. But, I'm sure you all would have handled the situation if it had gotten out of hand."

"You got that right," Miss Fanny agreed.

There were a few nods of assent, but most of the ladies looked at each other skeptically.

"Why, aren't you just a well of strength!" Viola snarled at Autumn hatefully. "You're just chocked full of inspiration."

Miss Fanny was taken aback by the venomous outburst. "Viola! Shame on you! It's not her fault you opened the door."

That really set Viola off. "Don't tell me that I'm the only one who can see through little Miss Sunshine! Oh, she was so quiet and pious when all of us first met her, but she's turning out to be chock-full of surprises."

"And what do you mean by that?" Autumn seemed as puzzled by the woman's tirade as the others.

"I'll tell you what," Viola spat. "You've been *first lady* for over a year at CLUCK Baptist, but from what I've heard, not only do the rest of us first ladies in the city know nothing about you, but the members of your husband's church don't know much more. On top of that, according to *you*, no one here is showing a 'spirit of cooperation'— except *you*, of course."

"Well, that's true," Miss Fanny confirmed.

"Ha!" Viola scoffed. "I don't buy the goody-two-shoes act. What about the walk she took out in the dark by herself the day we arrived? The rest of us were scared out of our minds about how dark it was around here."

Miss Fanny shrugged. "So?"

"It's just strange, that's all. I tell you there are a lot of strange things that happen when this woman is around.

Some of her church members have told me that she doesn't volunteer around the church like the first Mrs. Randall. She never helps on the bake sales, or cooks a dish for any church dinners. Then she gets here and has her own bag of spices, no less."

Miss Fanny was fed up with her babbling. "What is your point, Viola? Have you lost what little mind you got? You haven't said one thing that makes a bit of sense."

Viola was fuming. "I have *not* lost my mind. I've been wondering if the women at this retreat have. Look at her! What does an attractive woman like that see in a man nearly twice her age? She could have any man she wants. In fact, she thinks I didn't notice how cozy she was with George Handy."

"Who?" Miss Fanny questioned.

"The dead bus driver," Viola shot back.

"George Hadley," Miss Fanny corrected.

"Handy, Hadley, whatever his name was, she was throwing herself at him when we got off the bus and went to lunch. I know I'm not the only one who noticed it." She looked at the others expectantly.

Connie rolled her eyes. "Are you kidding? We've got some serious business going on around here and this is what you're wasting our time with?"

Some of the women nodded their heads in agreement with Connie while others tried to recall seeing anything transpiring between the young first lady and the deceased driver. Barely containing her rage, Autumn stepped forward to face Viola. Her voice was granite.

"Listen, lady, I try to get along with the people in my husband's church. I speak, I greet, and I mind my own business. As for what you *think* you saw between me and Mr. Hadley, I really don't care. But I do want to tell you one thing. For the rest of this retreat, I suggest you stay out of my face *and* out of my way."

Miss Fanny gave a nod of approval. "Well said."

The tension in the kitchen was interrupted by frantic shouts from the foyer. Back door business was instantly dismissed as the contingent of women—all except Viola— scurried to the front of the building. Miss Fanny and Autumn took up the rear, arriving in the foyer in time to see Bea peeking through the side window and shouting.

"Go ahead and call the police! It'll save us from calling them ourselves."

A gruff voice on the other side of the door hollered, "We're leaving, but you can believe we'll be back."

Bea turned to Connie. "They've got the nerve to threaten *us* just because you shot one of them."

Connie nodded. "He ought to be glad all I did was nick him."

"That's true." Bea nodded. "And since we can't call the police, if they do, we'll be rescued."

****

The claps of thunder were the only backdrop to Viola's furtive efforts as she tiptoed around the room that she shared with Miss Fanny, Lucretia, and Autumn. Instead of dashing to the front, she had veered to the room to see what she could find on that pious Autumn. There was something about that hussy that wasn't right, and she was going to find out what it was.

Dragging Autumn's suitcase from under the bed, she opened it, examining every compartment, quickly going through it. Nothing incriminating! Putting the suitcase back in place, the snooping continued as she moved to the dresser drawers and again found nothing. Likewise, she drew a blank after checking under the woman's mattress and in her pillow case.

Opening the wardrobe, she looked at the clothes hanging there. She had to admit that although Autumn's taste in clothing didn't meet her approval, the quality of her things was impressive. They were expensive and must be costing her husband a fortune. Many of the outfits hanging there were hardly appropriate for a preacher's wife, but she wasn't surprised.

Sorting through the assortment of garments, she checked the pockets of each piece of clothing coming up short until she reached into the pocket of a jacket. Slowly, she pulled an item from it and with knitted brow, examined it closely. *What was this about?*

As it began to dawn on her what she was holding in her hand, Viola's lips curled into a smile.

"Let's see you explain this, Miss High-and-Mighty."

CHAPTER 14

"I know you're not accusing this child of having anything to do with that bus driver's death." Miss Fanny looked Viola straight in her eyes, and placed both hands on her hips for emphasis. She meant for her stance to be threatening, and was ready to jump on this old cow any minute for coming up front and starting some mess.

Defiant, Viola stared Miss Fanny down.

"All I'm saying is the woman was the only one outside this building the night we came here and then the driver turned up dead."

An altercation between the two senior citizens seemed inevitable, so Bea quickly intervened.

"As a licensed private investigator, I feel…"

"When did you become a *licensed* PI?" Someone wanted to know. A growing murmur followed.

"Is she for real?"

"She told us earlier that she had some kind of license."

"I thought she was talking about a driver's license."

Bea ignored the doubters. "As I was *saying*, I feel that this kind of speculation is not only outrageous but dangerous."

"Ain't it the truth," Miss Fanny agreed. "*Somebody…*" She gave Viola the evil eye, "is in danger of getting a beat down…"

"Nobody is gonna be fighting in here." Hattie glared at her mother-in-law. "We are grown women, Christian women."

"Amen," Gladys interjected.

"And it says in the Bible, thou shall not kill." Viola directed the comment at Autumn.

"And it says in the law books that I can sue you for defamation of character," Autumn countered. "Now you say one more word."

"That's right," Connie was indignant. "The very idea of what you're trying to say, Viola, is disgraceful!"

Lucretia spoke up. "All she said was that Autumn was nowhere to be seen for a while, and the rest of us were in here!"

"And that's all she'd better say," Miss Fanny warned.

Some of the women agreed with Miss Fanny. Others were quite vocal about their suspicions and dislike of the glamorous first lady.

"And I'm saying that as a law official I go where the evidence leads!" Bea hollered over the noisy conflict. "There's no evidence."

Her words were drowned out in a melee of verbal insults as members of CLUCK Baptist vehemently defended their first lady. Once again, it was church against church. While the storm outside the conference center was dying down, the one inside the building was brewing with a vengeance until someone called out.

"Hey! What's that?"

Through the front window, an ominous red light was flashing in the distance. The ladies grew quiet as it came closer and closer.

Bea and some of the other women squinted through the glass in an attempt to make out the red glow.

"It looks like…"

"It is!"

"It's a police cruiser!"

Cheers replaced dissension.

"We're saved!"

****

The revolving light from the police car shining through the window was like manna from heaven to the women inside the conference center. The shouts of gratitude and praise could be heard by the two officers as they slogged through the downpour to the front door. Bea snatched it open before they could knock.

"Are we glad to see you!"

The uniformed officers entered the foyer, one tall, with a military bearing, the other one much shorter in stature with a confidence in his stride. Both were dripping wet. As they stood shaking water from their rain slickers, they were given a hero-like greeting by the women as the building vibrated with cheers. Everyone began to talk at once.

"We've got murderers stalking the center!" someone shouted at them over Bea's shoulder.

"They tried to break in."

"They wanted to kill us!"

"Go get the SWAT team!"

"Ladies! Ladies!" The older and taller of the officers raised his arms trying to calm the frenzy without success.

"Where's the rest of the cops?" asked Miss Fanny.

"Don't you guys have Uzis?" Pearl wanted to know.

The hysteria was reaching a crescendo when three men dressed in jeans, plaid shirts and sneakers stepped into the building behind the uniformed officers. The older man was stocky with steel gray eyes and thinning brown hair plastered to his round head. He appeared to be in his late forties, twice as old as his two companions, both lanky blonds, in their twenties. One sported long, stringy hair held back from his face by a rubber band. Unlike the officers, the trio wasn't wearing rain gear and they were drenched. Gradually, as the women began to recognize the men one by one, the noise among the women began to subside and there was a collective gasp.

Bea squealed. "That's them! That's them, officers! I saw them through the window!"

"And he's the one who tried to break in through the back door!" Connie pointed at the oldest member of the trio.

"There are murderers in the house!" Miss Fanny declared.

"You're damned right!" Connie's adversary responded in outrage. He pointed to her. "*She* tried to kill *me*!"

Among the women, hysteria turned to indignation.

"Liar!"

"Philistine!"

The situation threatened to turn ugly. Once again, the officers made an attempt to restore calm.

"Ladies, let me speak!" the older officer pleaded. "Please! Listen to me!"

The younger officer's approach was more direct. Taking a whistle out of his pocket, he blew it long and loud. The piercing sound caused some of the women to clamp their hands over their ears, but the chattering gradually decreased.

The older officer addressed the gathering. "Ladies, my name is Officer Renton, from the TCPD...."

"What is a TCPD?" Miss Fanny interrupted

"The Tri-County Police Department, ma'am," the young officer answered for him.

"Who are you?" Bea questioned. "You look like you're about sixteen."

"I'm Officer Simms, ma'am," he touched his hat slightly in salute. "And I'm twenty-two."

"I've got shoes older than you," Miss Fanny cracked.

Officer Renton intervened. "We received a call from these gentlemen…"

"Gentlemen?" Connie raised a skeptical brow.

"Yes ma'am. They said that someone in here assaulted them…."

"Assault?" Hattie questioned.

"Yes, assault. Allegedly someone took a shot at one of them, and drew blood." Officer Renton's gaze fell on Connie.

The uproar among the women started again. The wind had shifted. Now it was the church ladies versus the accusers.

"Didn't nobody assault nobody!"

"Oh, yeah?" the older camper pointed to his ear with a blood smeared hand. "Who did this?"

"We can show you assault!" Miss Fanny warned.

"Bring it on, old lady!" one of the young men declared.

"Old lady?" Miss Fanny reared back and balled her fist. "You'll see what this old lady can do!"

While Hattie restrained her mother-in-law, barbs and insults flew between the two sides.

"Officer Renton scowled. "Hold it! Hold it. Or I'll lock all of you up!"

"I hope you're referring to them, too?" Bea pointed to the three men.

"He's the man who tried to force his way in through the back door," Connie nodded toward the older one.

"All of these men tried to break in, Officer," Bea informed Renton. "Who knows what would have happened if they had gotten inside. We were defending ourselves!"

"It was raining cats and dogs," one of the younger men shouted.

"We were trying to get shelter." The other one was just as aggravated.

"There was a tornado warning." The oldest of the trio addressed Officer Renton. "And that woman shot at me for trying to save our lives." He pointed to Connie again before rubbing his ear.

"That's because you tried to break in here and murder us all," Hattie barked.

"We had to beat him back out of the door," Dorothy tried to explain.

The older camper pounced on her statement. "See, Officer! I told you. It was assault and battery with intent to kill. Some of these old biddies were trying to stab me with knives and that broad tried to shoot my ear off! I'm pressing charges." He glowered at Connie. "I want her arrested, and I want her arrested *now*! If you don't do it, I'm making a citizen's arrest. I want her ass thrown in jail!"

CHAPTER 15

The uproar made by the women over the camper's demand that Connie be arrested was so intense that for a moment the rough looking campers were concerned. Everyone was bellowing, and barking at the men at once. The noise was deafening.

"Ladies! Quiet!" Officer Renton implored.

At 6' 5", he was a big man, a former marine used to giving commands. His graveled voice and intimidating size usually brought instant compliance to any demand he made, but not now. He was being completely ignored.

Undaunted, he placed his fingers in his mouth, stretched it to distortion and released a whistle that could be heard in the next county. The noise ceased.

"Ladies, calm down!" Officer Renton ordered. "Let's start over." He nodded toward the stocky grey-eyed man. "This is Mr. Buddy Coolpix, and his nephew, Jerry." The stringy blond with the ponytail looked at the women threateningly. "And this is his other nephew, Walter, Jerry's brother."

Walter resembled a clean cut, college student with his blond buzz cut, but the bare arms he sported under the sleeves of his rolled-up shirt challenged that assumption. He had a tattoo on each arm. One depicted a dagger, dripping blood droplets that spelled the word 'stud'. On the other arm a snake slithered up to his elbow bearing the word 'deadly'. His piercing, blue eyes looked at Connie as though he wanted the viper on his arm to strike. Connie returned his intense stare.

Taking a notebook out of his pocket, Officer Renton flipped it open. "Now, all of you have had a lot to say, but I need to know who I'm talking to. Who's the spokesperson for this group?"

Without fanfare, and without waiting on consensus, Bea spoke up. "I am, Mrs. Bea Bell, and if you think you're going to take Connie out of here…"

"Connie?" Officer Renton raised a brow.

"That's me," Connie raised a single finger to distinguish herself from the other women. "My name is Mrs. Connie Palmer…"

"She's the owner of Palmer Realty, in Indianapolis," Bea huffed. "She's a *very* successful business woman and highly respected member in the community. Mrs. Palmer knows lots of important people in the state capitol, as do I." She stabbed a finger at him to emphasis her point. "So, if you think you're going to arrest her you've got another think coming!"

"I'll call the wrath of God and all of his angels down on you if you try it," Hattie warned.

"Oh, really?" Officer Renton raised a brow. "And who are you?"

Drawing up to her full 5 feet 8 inch height, Hattie answered haughtily. "I am Mrs. Hattie Collier, owner and founder of Half Way Home Funeral Consulting Services." Reaching into her pocket, she withdrew a card and, much to the surprise of the officer, she pressed it in his hand.

"When death is at your door, call on me."

Miss Fanny pointed at the Coolpixs. "I can't believe that you're gonna listen to what these murderers have to say over a house full of decent, law abiding, church going *Christian* women!" There were mummers of agreement among the ladies.

"Why do you keep calling *us* murderers?" asked the pony-tailed, Jerry. "*She's* the one who tried to kill my Uncle Bud!" He turned his malevolent glare on Connie.

Rolling her eyes at him, she turned to Renton. "While you're so intent on arresting *me*, maybe you need to get out to that bus that brought us here and examine the driver's body."

"Body?" Officer Renton looked confused.

"What body?" The Coolpixs and Officer Simms spoke simultaneously.

"The dead one that the three of *them* left on the bus down the road," Bea declared.

"She's talking out of her head!" Uncle Bud shouted. "My nephews and me don't know a damn thing about a body."

"This is some sort of scam to get *her*," Jerry pointed to Connie, "out of being arrested!"

"Oh! So you're saying that we're a bunch of liars!" an irate Dorothy yelled from the crowd. Her comment was followed by a chorus of angry mumbling.

Bea spoke with confidence. "I can assure you, Officer Renton, that you will not find one single criminal in this group. We came here for a weekend retreat, and while some of us were trying to go on a peaceful walk in the woods, we stumbled across our driver..."

"And he had been murdered," Hattie finished.

"Murdered?" Officer Renton looked skeptical.

"That's right, and *I* found the body," Gladys informed him proudly.

"You are?" Officer Simms stood poised to write.

"Mrs. Gladys Hodges. I'm a member of Twelve Disciples Christian Church."

"Actually, *I* found the body," Bea corrected. "Gladys found the bus."

"And we think *they* killed the body on the bus!" Hattie pointed an accusing finger at the three men.

"You're a bunch of lying hags!" Uncle Bud hollered, jabbing a finger at Hattie that threatened to resume the verbal battle between the warring factions.

"Let's stop the name calling on both sides, folks," Officer Renton demanded. "I need facts."

Bea was getting perturbed. "The *fact* is we're the victims here and I can prove it. My son is a lieutenant in the Indianapolis Police Department. If one of you officers has a cell phone, I'll call him and he can vouch for everyone of us."

"Can't do that ma'am, "Officer Simms replied, unmoved and unimpressed by her request. "You'll have to use your own phone."

"We don't have our cell phones." Hattie gave Dorothy and Thelma each a pointed look.

Thelma explained to the officers. "We forgot and left them back in Indianapolis."

"You mean you ladies are alone out here with no means of communication?" Renton's brow knitted. "That's not too smart."

"That's why we didn't want to let these three strangers in the building!" Connie declared. "We're like sitting ducks in here."

"And we were forced to defend ourselves against these predators!" Bea added dramatically, ignoring the angry reaction of the three men to her description of them. "So, please let me call my son. His name is Lieutenant Bryant

Bell and he'll clear this mess up. We'll see who the criminals are then." She shot the campers a look of scorn.

Officer Renton denied the request again. "No can do."

Bea puffed up like a peacock. "Well, let me tell you, as a certified Private Investigator, I *know*, the law."

Neither Officer Renton nor Simms looked convinced. The three campers laughed out loud. Bea wasn't dissuaded.

"The law clearly states that when under arrest a suspect gets at least one telephone…"

"Nobody has said you're a suspect, ma'am. We never said anybody is under arrest." Officer Sims appeared amused.

"*She* ought to be!" Uncle Bud loudly interjected, indicating Connie.

His comment sent the women into another uproar. Barbs and insults resumed.

"This from a stalker?"

"He's a stalker, a murderer, *and* a liar."

"And the truth ain't in him."

"Okay! Okay! There's an easy way to settle this," Renton's booming voice rose above the din. "You three," he pointed to Bea, Hattie and Gladys, "Come and show me where this body is supposed to be." He pointed to the Coolpix trio. "You three sit right here in the lobby. No straying." He turned to his colleague, Simms. "Joe, you stay here and play referee. Make sure the rest of these women don't cross that threshold." He drew an invisible line between the tiled foyer and the hallway. Officer Simms started waving the women backward.

"All right! You heard what he said. All of you go to your rooms."

Whether it was his tone, or being ordered around by this pint sized, junior officer, his demand hit a nerve among some of the women. They made their objections loud and clear.

"Go to our bedrooms!"

"What are we, children?"

"I'm old enough to be your grand... your mother!"

Officer Renton stopped Connie as she made her retreat. "And you, Mrs. Palmer." He held his hand out. "Give me the piece."

Connie looked from his stern face to his hand and back again. "A piece of what?"

"Your gun, Connie, your gun," Bea mumbled out of the side of her mouth. She was so embarrassed. How could Connie investigate crime and not know the simplest weapons slang? They had to talk.

Reaching into her jacket pocket, Connie withdrew her gun and gave it to the officer. He took a plastic bag from seemingly nowhere and held it out to her. She slipped the firearm inside and retreated down the hallway with the other women.

"That looks like an evidence bag to me." Bea looked at Renton suspiciously.

Zipping it up, the officer didn't address Bea's statement. Instead, he looked at his note book.

"Mrs. Bell, Mrs. Collier and Mrs. Hodges," he nodded toward the front door, "come show me this body you're talking about."

****

Bea didn't like the woods at night. When she, Hattie and Dorothy were walking back to the conference center in the rain, she couldn't see her hand in front of her face.

Except for the eerie shine of the patrol car's headlights on the narrow road ahead, the experience wasn't any better now than it had been a few hours earlier. There was nothing but blackness surrounding them. The wet foliage emitted a smell of decay. Everything looked and felt sinister.

They were silent as they drove along in the patrol car. Bea, Hattie and Gladys sat in the back seat. The amber glow of the dashboard in front was the only light in the interior. Bea was sitting between Gladys and Hattie, who were huddled against their respective doors. Bea could sense that both women were tense. So was she.

"I don't like this," Bea whispered.

"Me either," Gladys and Hattie echoed simultaneously.

"Don't worry ladies," Officer Renton's voice drifted back to them from the front seat. "You're with me, and I'm armed."

Bea rolled her eyes at him. *That's reassuring.* She hoped that he could feel her skepticism. How dare this man deny her the right to call her son! Wait until she got back to Indianapolis.

The ladies continued to peer into the darkness when suddenly the looming sight of the abandoned bus appeared. The squad car came to a stop. Opening the glove compartment, Officer Renton withdrew a flashlight, turned it on and proceeded to get out of the car.

"You three wait here." He slammed the door behind him and started walking toward the bus.

"What did he think? We're going to make a break for it in the dark?" Bea cracked. This man would *never* get back in her good graces.

"This is a nightmare!" There were tears in Gladys' voice.

"*Him* or this situation?" asked Hattie.

Gladys gave a shaky sigh. "Both."

The women watched as Officer Renton vanished into the night. The illumination from the flashlight helped them monitor his progress. They followed the beam of light as the officer boarded the vehicle, and knew from its dance in the darkness the moment Renton spotted George Hadley. For a second, the light remained frozen in place, and then disappeared.

"He's stooping down to examine the body," Bea explained.

"And I bet he thinks *we* murdered him." Hattie emitted a heavy sigh.

"And now we're out here in these God forsaken woods like lambs going to slaughter," Gladys said shakily, peering anxiously into the darkness. She checked the car lock.

"Well, we know we didn't do it," Bea grumbled. "The most likely suspects are sitting back at the center."

The glow of light reappeared through the bus windows. It illuminated the driver's seat and then disappeared again. Suddenly, the surrounding woods were bright as the exterior and interior lights on the bus came on.

Gladys started. "Bea, I thought you said the bus wouldn't start!"

"It wouldn't. According to Dorothy the battery was dead."

Hattie was totally confused. "Car lights don't come on when the battery is dead. Everybody knows that."

"Apparently, Dorothy doesn't," Bea said.

They could see Officer Renton sitting in the driver's seat, trying to start the vehicle. *Nothing.*

Getting off the bus, he used the lights from the squad car to guide him back to the vehicle. He slid inside.

"Well, Officer?" Bea inquired. "Didn't we tell you? What do you think?"

"I *think* I have a murder on my hands."

"See!" A triumphant Bea felt vindicated. Maybe this bonehead would finally listen. "After we found the body, some of my friends and I tried to drive to town to get the authorities to help us, but the bus stopped and we couldn't get it started again. Does going for help sound like something that murderers would do?" Bea folded her arms tightly, waiting for an apology.

Officer Renton turned slowly in his seat. In the shadows of the car's interior, the women couldn't see his eyes, but they could sense his agitation.

"Did you say that some of you moved the bus, with the body on it, Mrs. Bell? In other words, you tampered with a crime scene."

Looking guilty, Bea's eyes slid sideward to Hattie and Gladys. Both stared straight ahead, looking as if they wanted to disappear.

Bea swallowed hard. *You have the right to remain silent,* reverberated though her head. It occurred to her that perhaps for once in her life she should just shut up.

CHAPTER 16

Most of the ladies had complied with Officer Simms' command to retreat to their rooms. A small contingent remained clustered in the hallway, staring at Uncle Bud and his nephews.

In Miss Fanny's room, Connie paced from one end to the other, still upset about what had happened in the foyer. "I can't believe that man took my gun. Those three jerks stalk *us* and because I fought for our lives *I'm* in trouble."

"You didn't do a thing wrong," Miss Fanny assured her. "Don't worry. Those murderers are bound to get theirs."

"This whole trip has been a nightmare," Lucretia moaned. "I'm ready to take my behind home, right now."

"You ain't spoke nothing but the truth," Miss Fanny agreed. Getting up from her bed, she removed her earrings and angrily tossed them on the dresser. Abruptly, she turned to Lucretia. "Let's do it. Let's leave this place."

Lucretia's eyes lit up. "I'm with you."

Connie looked at the two women in astonishment. "Have you gone crazy? There's no way you can go home now."

"We'll see about that!" declared Miss Fanny. "Let's go, Lucretia."

Together the unlikely allies filed out of the room

Connie scrambled after them. "I'm not about to miss this!"

The three women marched past the curious faces of the ladies still lingering in the hall, including Viola. The trio started to enter the foyer where Officer Simms was keeping an eye on the Coolpix crew. The officer's hand went up immediately, halting their progress.

"Ladies! Stop right there."

Miss Fanny growled, "We want to talk to you."

"Well, you can do that from the hallway. You're in the no cross zone." He drew the same imaginary line that had been drawn earlier. "Your place is right over there." He glowered at them as they inched backward, reluctantly.

Miss Fanny was fuming. "See here, young man, me and my friend ain't as young as we used to be and we need to go home."

"Yeah," Lucretia agreed, trying not to show surprise at having Miss Fanny refer to her as a friend.

Deciding to use all the ammunition she had in her arsenal, Miss Fanny reverted to her little old lady card. Boldly crossing the make believe line, she walked slowly toward the officer. "Lucretia and me are the oldest ones in this building. We don't know how much more time we got on this earth."

"Sorry to hear that, ma'am," Simms said, unmoved. "And what is your point, exactly?"

Lucretia picked up the appeal. "It ought to be as plain as the nose on your face that women our age had nothing to do with that murder."

Getting no response, the two determined women forged ahead. It was Lucretia's turn to try the age card.

"We can go at any time and we'd like to do it at home with our families. We sure can't afford to get tangled up in something like this."

"Why don't you give the two of us a ride out of these woods?" Miss Fanny suggested.

"Take us to the station and we'll catch a bus back to Indianapolis," Lucretia assured him.

Chuckling, the young officer shook his head at their audacity. "You two do have nerve, I'll give you credit for that. But, I'm not taking you anywhere, ladies. Or *you* either." He scowled at Connie, who remained in the hallway.

She threw her hands up in mock surrender. "I haven't said a thing."

His attitude didn't deter Miss Fanny, who suddenly had a revelation. "Come to think of it, Officer, you don't have to take us anywhere. That groundskeeper who let us in this place will be here tomorrow. He can take us out of here."

Lucretia brightened. "That's right!"

"I'll be damned!" Uncle Bud jumped to his feet. "You old farts are in this together. You're not shooting at me and getting away that easy."

His words revived the dissension. Not only did Miss Fanny and Lucretia turn on him, but so did the hallway loiterers. The taunts and jeers were relentless, and Miss Fanny gave Uncle Bud a stern warning.

"You got one more time to make a comment like that and you're gonna wish Connie had shot you."

The raised voices brought several of the other ladies out of their rooms to see what the commotion was about. They got there just in time to hear Officer Simms' declaration.

"You all may as well simmer down. I don't know what's going on around here but if my partner discovers there really is a body on that bus, you're all potential suspects. That means nobody is going anywhere."

"You've got that right," Officer Renton said, walking through the front door just as Simms was speaking. Bea, Hattie, and Gladys were with him. "Everybody is staying right here. We've got questions for you." He turned to his partner. "Like they said, there's a body out there. We're going to need backup on this one."

"You mean you're going to call in your entire Goon Squad on a group of harmless Christian women?" Miss Fanny questioned.

"We *are* the *Goon Squad* for this area," Renton shot back, "and in this area, folks don't go around killing their neighbors. This is a law-abiding community."

Officer Simms leveled Connie with a look. "And neighbors don't shoot at innocent people either."

"I bet they do when the *neighbors* are trying to break into their house," Connie shot back.

Simms ignored her and addressed Renton, "I'll go to the squad car and see if I can raise Willie."

The younger officer exited the front door. Officer Renton turned to the ladies.

"While he tries to get a hold of our volunteer deputy, let's see if we can sort this thing out."

Having joined the other ladies standing in the hallway, Bea let out a derisive snort. "*Volunteer* deputy? I assure you, Officer, we won't appreciate being drilled like criminals even if you bring your *entire* department here."

The chorus of amen and hallelujahs of agreement were plentiful. Officer Renton didn't appear to be concerned as he flashed Bud a crooked smile.

"Now suppose you tell me how you and your nephews happen to be out here in the middle of the woods, Mr. Coolpix. I may have missed that little detail in all of the confusion."

Bea, standing next to Connie, whispered to her. "Coolpix? That's a strange name. I bet it's phony."

Bud ran his fingers through his thinning hair and gave a frustrated sigh. "Like I told you when you picked us up on the road, we're campers, and we decided to come to the woods for the weekend."

Renton took a quick glance at Bud's muddy shoes, and he scratched his chin thoughtfully. "I see, and where do the three of you live?

"Over near Bean Blossom," the tattooed Walter answered.

Renton grunted. "Really? Where *exactly* near Bean Blossom do you live?"

Walter threw a look at his uncle, who intervened.

"The boys don't exactly live near Bean Blossom," Bud corrected. "They see the sign a lot when we drive around."

"Yeah, we just moved up here from Evansville," Walter explained, "and we don't know our way around yet."

"Bean Blossom is a colorful name," Jerry added. "It's hard to forget."

"The boys are staying with me," said Bud. "I got a place near Mooresville."

Officer Renton nodded slowly. "So the three of you *might* live in Brown County, or you *might* live in Morgan County. How long have your nephews been in this part of the country, Mr. Coolpix?

"Two weeks."

"And how old are you, Jerry?"

"Twenty-five," the pony-tailed brother looked as though he was confused by the question.

"And you Walter?"

"Twenty-one." The question didn't appear to faze him.

A frown creased Officer Renton's face. "It seems to me that you boys have been here long enough and you're old enough to know where you live."

"He's got them now!" Connie murmured excitedly to Bea.

Without giving them time to respond, Renton fired a question in Bud's direction. "About what time did you get here?"

"I told you in the squad car, as soon as we heard the tornado warning on our weather radio, we made our way over here."

"I'm not asking about *here* to the conference center. When did you get to the woods?"

"Around five o'clock." Walter Coolpix answered this time. His bother and uncle bobbed their heads in agreement.

"Didn't you know about the tornado watch before you set out?

Bud spoke up. "Look, we didn't decide to go camping until late. Besides, if there's some kind of a murder, we're not the ones who did it. We don't go around stabbing people. You don't have a thing on us and if we're not under arrest then we don't have to answer any more questions. After all, I'm the victim here."

Connie heard Bea gasp. "What's wrong?"

Bea signaled Connie to follow her down the hallway. Reluctant to leave a good vantage point, Connie relented. Along the way Bea grabbed Hattie by the arm, forcing her to come along. Officer Simms walked in the front door before they could get away.

"Where do you three ladies think you're going?" he barked.

"I've got to talk with my friends, "Bea tossed over her shoulder never breaking stride.

"Stop right there!" The officer left no room for debate. "You aren't going anywhere until we say you can go. "

"He's right about that," Renton agreed with his subordinate, before asking him about their backup. "Did you get him?"

"He should be here shortly."

Renton looked relieved. "Let's hope. Maybe with the three of us we might be able get through all of this quicker."

He bent and whispered something in Simms ear. The two men then looked from the cluster of ladies to the trio huddled on the bench. Officer Renton returned his attention to the women.

"Okay, ladies, I know it's been a long night, and you're tired, so I want *all* of you to clear this hall and go back to your rooms. My deputy and I will be calling on some of you soon." He turned to the campers. "As for you three, I'll be talking to you one at a time." He pointed to Bud Coolpix. "You first. In there." He motioned Uncle Bud into a library that was to the right of the front door. Then he pointed to another open door. "Jerry and Walter, you two go in that office. Close the door and wait. I want this lobby and hallway cleared."

The three men followed directions without protest. Renton joined Bud, closing the door behind them. Grumbling, the women drifted back down the hall and into their quarters. Once again, Officer Simms stood as a sentinel in what was the forbidden zone.

On their way back to their rooms, Bea hustled Hattie and Connie into a nearby meeting room. Shutting the door softly, so the sound wouldn't be heard, she locked it.

Connie looked puzzled. "What's up with you?"

Bea was breathless with excitement. "Do either of you remember us saying anything to those three campers about the driver being stabbed?"

Hattie squinted hard, trying to recall past conversations. "I don't remember saying anything." She gave Connie a quizzical look.

"Me either? Why?"

"Because when Officer Renton was asking them questions, that Uncle Bud character said that they weren't guilty of *stabbing* anyone. How did he know the driver was stabbed?"

Hattie's eyes lit up. "That proves it! I knew they looked guilty! Only a killer would draw a bloody dagger on his arm!"

Connie's face was flushed. "That cinches it! "

"I know," Bea agreed, "but I'm not sure Officer Renton picked up on it. I knew he'd need our help in this investigation."

The women jumped, startled by a loud knock on the door. It was followed by the strident voice of Officer Simms. "Who's in there?"

Unlocking the door, Bea peeked out and said sweetly, "Yes?"

"Are Mrs. Collier and Mrs. Palmer in there with you?"

"Yes, they are."

"We need you up front, ladies. My partner wants to talk to the three of you."

"Why?" Hattie came up behind Bea and peered over her shoulder. "You'll just be wasting your time. "Hadley might have been a pain in the butt, but we didn't kill him."

"We still need to question you." Swinging the door open, Simms motioned for the women to follow him.

When they entered the foyer, Officer Renton was standing outside the library door.

Connie addressed both officers. "This is silly. We had no reason to kill that driver."

"I thought you were questioning the campers?" Bea wasn't pleased at all about having been summoned.

Renton's eyes narrowed. "I'll be asking the questions here." Turning to Simms, he nodded toward the office door. "Go in there and tell them to come out. I'll get their uncle." Renton opened the library door.

"Get out here."

Simms retrieved the brothers. Uncle Bud exited his room the same time as Jerry and Walter. Renton directed all three back to the bench which they had first occupied. He then fixed his gaze on the women.

"Mrs. Bell and Mrs. Collier, I decided that since you were the first to find the body, I need to talk to the two of you. Our deputy has arrived and, he'll cover the entrance." He turned to the trio of men. "Officer Simms will be talking with you two brothers, one at a time, in the library." He transferred his attention back to the ladies. "I'll be talking with you, Mrs. Bell and you, Mrs. Collier in the office. Mrs. Palmer, you can go back to your room until I need you."

Before the women could protest, the front door to the conference center opened and in walked the unassuming groundskeeper who had welcomed them and helped them get settled. The ladies were more than happy to see him.

"Mr. Lucas!" Hattie squealed with relief.

All three women looked at him hopefully. Maybe he could help get them out of here, and back home. Renton greeted him with a nod.

"Glad you could make it Deputy Lucas."

Deputy Lucas! The women were stunned. The groundskeeper was the volunteer deputy!

CHAPTER 17

At first glance—at any glance—no one would have guessed that Mr. Lucas had the slightest connection to law enforcement. As the ladies had observed on first meeting him, the man had an uncanny resemblance to the character, Barney Fife, on the old Andy Griffith TV series. He was short for a man, maybe 5'7", and so thin that he looked emaciated. If it wasn't for the leather belt he wore, cinched to the last hole, the grey pants he wore beneath his green rain slicker might have fallen to his ankles. His lean chest seemed to swim in the oversized cotton shirt he wore. His elongated face was pale and far from handsome. His dark brown eyes were too close. His eyebrows were too bushy and a breath away from being a uni-brow. He had a long hawk-like nose and lips so thin they resembled a straight line across his face. To top it off, when he removed the faded Pacers baseball cap he wore, his light brown hairline was receding. It was difficult to guess his age, maybe in his forties or early fifties.

Hanging his wet rain coat and his jacket on a rack by the door, he acknowledged the women with a polite nod. "Ladies"

He was met with a scattering of passive greetings, with the exception of Bea. She couldn't believe that this mild mannered little man was Renton's other deputy.

"You have got to be kidding! Mr. Lucas, I thought you said you were the grounds keeper!"

"I am ma'am," he acknowledged quietly.

Bea whirled on Officer Renton. "And you've got *him* helping you on this case? I'd like to know what kind of qualifications does *he* have to be part of this investigation. I'm a licensed Private Detective, a graduate of the Get Your Man Institute for Private Eyes."

Renton raised a dubious brow. "The Get Your Man Institute for Private Eyes?"

"That's right." Bea's tone could freeze ice. "I've got a license in my purse to prove it. What kind of license does *he* have? What kind of training does *he* have?" She turned to the groundskeeper. "No offense, Mr. Lucas."

"None taken, and to answer your question I do have an Associate's degree in criminal justice. I've been a volunteer with the department for a couple of years now."

"I see." Bea folded her arms tightly. "And just what does a *volunteer* deputy do?"

"Whatever I tell him to," Officer Renton declared before answering his ringing cell phone.

As Renton spoke to his caller, the women remained clustered in the hallway entrance whispering about Mr. Lucas. After disconnecting, Renton addressed Officer Simms.

"There's been a change in plans. That was the coroner. He's headed to the crime scene and I've got to meet him there. You go ahead and question the Coolpixs and see what you can get out of them." He turned to Mr. Lucas. "Willie, I'm stationing you here in the lobby to make sure nobody leaves."

"And just where are we supposed to go, with no transportation?" Connie wondered aloud.

"Nowhere!" Officer Renton said pointedly, his patience waning. "And when I get back, I *will* be questioning you." He turned to Bea. "And you." His gaze fell on Hattie. "And *you*." He started to leave.

Bea called after him. "When you get back, we'd still like to help you solve this case."

Renton slammed the front door firmly behind him, never looking back.

"He is so arrogant," Connie complained.

"He's only doing his job," Mr. Lucas assured her, an enigmatic smile plastered on his face. "And he's good at it too."

"Okay ladies, you can go back to your rooms now," Simms called to them. "Willie, I'll be in the library questioning these men one at a time. Make sure the women stay back there and that these two..." He motioned to the uncle and his oldest nephew, "stay put. Jerry, you follow me."

Mr. Lucas took a seat in the lobby. The women started drifting down the hallway to their rooms. Bea, Hattie and Connie were following the other ladies when the door to Miss Fanny's room suddenly opened and she gestured frantically for the trio to come inside.

"Get in here!" Grabbing her daughter-in-law, she pulled her by the arm.

Hattie protested. "What in the world? Stop manhandling me!"

"Shush!" Miss Fanny put a silencing finger to her lips. After hustling the women inside, she stuck her head out of the door and checked the hall. Satisfied that the coast was clear, she shut the door. Autumn Randall was sitting on her bed looking worried. Miss Fanny seemed just as anxious.

Hattie's eyes shifted from the young woman to the older one. "What is wrong with you two?"

Ya'll won't believe what's going on!" Miss Fanny flopped down in a chair. Her eyes were as round as saucers.

"Bea gave her a bewildered frown. "You look like you've seen a ghost."

"No, it's more like we've heard one," Autumn quipped.

"What are you talking about?" Connie sat down on Miss Fanny's bed.

"I'm talking about *that*." Miss Fanny pointed down toward Connie's feet. All eyes turned in that direction.

"What are we looking at?" Bea asked. "The carpet?"

Miss Fanny shook her head. "The air vent."

Hattie gave an irritated sigh. "What about the air vent?"

"And where's Lucretia and Viola?" Connie wanted to know.

"They're probably somewhere around here stirring up trouble," Miss Fanny snapped. "Forget them. Now back to the vent…"

"As far as we can figure out, our bedroom shares it with that office up front," Autumn explained.

Hattie looked confused. "Shares what?"

"The vent!" Miss Fanny, Connie and Bea answered simultaneously.

Hattie shrugged. "So?"

"For some reason you can *hear* through that thing," Miss Fanny said excitedly, "and you can hear really good, if it's quiet in this room."

Bea was growing impatient "Miss Fanny, we've got a murder to solve. Can you get to the point?"

Autumn did that for her. What she had to say got the attention of all three of the amateur sleuths.

"We heard something through that vent that might solve the bus driver's murder."

Bea, Hattie and Connie exchanged doubtful looks before returning their attention to the women.

"Why don't the two of you start at the beginning," Bea suggested.

"Baby, go guard that door so Viola and Lucretia can't barge in here and get all in our business," Miss Fanny directed Autumn. The young woman did as asked and stood against the unlocked door. Satisfied, Miss Fanny turned to Hattie.

"Let me ask the three of you something. You just came from the lobby. Did you see who was in that room next to the library?"

Hattie nodded. "Nobody's in it now, but the two younger campers came out of it, Harry and Waldo…"

"Jerry and Walter," Connie corrected. "I think the officers put them in there to question them."

"Well, we didn't hear anybody being questioned," Miss Fanny said. "But, we sure heard an earful."

"Yes, Lord," Autumn agreed.

"Tell us what happened, Miss Fanny," Bea prompted.

"You say there's nobody in the room now?" Miss Fanny glanced down at the vent.

"No," Connie reassured her. "When we came back here two of the men were on the bench in the lobby and Officer Simms was taking the other one in the library."

Bea interjected. "It turns out that guy who let us in the center, Mr. Lucas…"

"The groundskeeper?" Autumn sat up happily sensing rescue.

"One in the same, but it turns out he's not here to save us. He's some sort of volunteer deputy under Officer

Renton," Bea informed her. "He's sitting in the foyer guarding them as well as us."

"Hmmmm," Miss Fanny pondered this latest development, and then shrugged. "All right, but let me tell you what happened while ya'll was out there. I was lying in here, minding my own business, happy as a lark that Lucretia and big mouth Viola weren't in the room. I was enjoying the quiet, when all of a sudden I hear this noise. It sounded like loud whispering. At first I thought it was someone outside the door, but it wasn't coming from that direction. So I laid there and listened some more…"

"Okay, so what were you listening to?" Hattie urged. Her mother-in-law could be so dramatic.

Not appreciating being rushed, Miss Fanny gave a dismissive wave of her hand. "Do ya'll want to hear this or not?"

"Don't pay attention to her." Bea threw Hattie a warning look. "Go on."

"Thank you, Bea." She rolled her eyes at Hattie. "As I was saying, I laid there and listened and realized that the sounds were coming from there." She pointed to the vent. "There were two voices, both of them male, so I knew it had to be either the deputies or them Cool people…"

"Coolpix," Connie corrected.

"Whatever. Anyway, it didn't take long to figure out it was them. They were talking about how they were scared that the officers would find out what they were really doing in these woods."

"What was that?" Bea perked up.

"According to one of them, they were 'looking at opportunities for growth development'."

"For *what?*" Hattie looked puzzled.

Autumn jumped into the conversation. "That's when I came into the room. Miss Fanny shushed me and whispered to me to listen. We both put our ears to the grate. From what they were saying they had been out here in the woods *pretending* that they were camping, but what they were really doing was looking for an isolated place to grow marijuana…"

"Marijuana!" The three sleuths echoed.

Miss Fanny took up the tale. "That's right, *marijuana*! Weed! They're dope dealers! From what we heard, them scoundrels have been growing weed on that so called farm of theirs and they're looking to expand!"

"Can you believe it? They're bold enough to be looking for a place somewhere in *these* woods—a state park!" Autumn was as astonished as the others.

"If *that* ain't nerve." Hattie was flabbergasted. "I've heard it all!"

"Oh, no you haven't," Miss Fanny assured her. "You see when it started storming, it turns out these *campers* didn't know how to put their tent up and when it blew away they had to look for shelter."

"It seems the *geniuses* got lost in the woods and couldn't even find their car," Autumn sneered.

Bea was also amused. "Sounds like they've got more corn sense than common sense."

"It gets better," Autumn assured her. "Miss Fanny will you do the honors?"

"So these three bozos were stumbling through the woods looking for where they parked…"

"They had a map but it got wet and tore apart," Autumn interrupted.

"The lightening was striking all around them," Miss Fanny described vividly, "and they're out there with all those trees and no shelter, when what do you think they saw?"

"The conference center!" Bea blurted, caught up in the story.

"No fool! The bus! The bus that brought us here!" Miss Fanny grinned triumphantly at the looks of shock on the women's faces. Autumn's neck was swiveling up and down like a bobble head doll.

Bea leaped off the bed. She was so excited she began walking in circles.

"This means that they did it! We've got the proof that they did it! They killed the driver! We got them!"

The grin on Miss Fanny's face vanished. "What *we*? I know you mean *we* as in *me* and Autumn."

Bea shrugged. "This is no time to nitpick…"

Suddenly, Autumn stumbled forward as someone tried to open the door she was blocking.

"Hey!" Viola shrilled from the other side. "What's blocking the door?"

"What's going on in there?" Lucretia inquired.

They knocked and banged while Autumn resisted their entry until Miss Fanny gestured for her to let them enter. Slowly, Autumn opened the door.

Viola and Lucretia stood in the doorway looking upset. Several women stood behind them.

Viola's eyes roamed the room, looking suspiciously at the women occupying its interior. "What's going on in here? What are you all up to?" Her gaze fell on Miss Fanny. "Lucretia and me paid for this room too, what gives you the right to keep us out of here? What are ya'll in here doing?"

Miss Fanny came to her feet and faced Viola. "Well, for your information, what we're *doing* is solving the bus driver's murder."

Viola cackled. "Is that a fact?"

The commotion in the hallway brought the volunteer deputy to the door. "What's all this noise about?"

"It's about murder, Mr. Lucas," Miss Fanny told him. "It's about telling the truth about who killed our bus driver, George Hadley. We know who did it."

Mr. Lucas raised a surprised brow. "Oh really?"

"Yes *really?*" Viola asked sarcastically. "Because while you've been locked in here trying to *guess* who did it. *I* figured out who the murderer really is."

Miss Fanny cackled. "And who do *you* think *did it,* Miss Smart Aleck?"

A predatory smile crossed Viola's face as her eyes slowly surveyed the room and stopped. She pointed at the accused culprit before speaking. "Autumn Randall."

CHAPTER 18

Bea, Connie, Hattie and Miss Fanny were shocked. Autumn Randall looked dumbfounded.

Miss Fanny was first to find her voice. "Viola, if you're not the craziest, most ornery heifer I've ever seen, then I don't know who is. How can you stand there and make such a foolish statement? Just because you can't get along with the woman don't mean you have the right to say something like that!"

"I'm not going to address your insults, Fanny Collier, because I'm not saying this because I don't like her. I'm saying it because it's true."

Her words were greeted with a derisive snort from Autumn. All eyes turned to the young minister's wife as her disdain turned to laughter.

"You see!" Viola cried triumphantly. "I knew I wasn't wrong about her. How cold do you have to be to kill a man and then laugh about it?"

Recovering from her laughing jag, Autumn stood with her shoulders squared and her fists clutched at her side. "Lady, you are crazy and you're making a fool of yourself. I didn't kill anyone, but at this point, I'm trying hard not to kill you."

"So now you're threatening me? One murder wasn't enough, and I've got proof of that one!"

"What proof?" One of the women in the hall asked.

"Proof that Autumn Randall killed the bus driver," Viola said over her shoulder.

A rumble of disbelief rippled through the gathering.

"Oh, my God!"

"Reverend Randall's wife killed the bus driver?"

"That sweet little thing?"

"That's nonsense, who said she did it?"

"Did she confess?"

Mr. Lucas appeared bewildered by the entire scenario. His hands shook slightly as he withdrew a notepad from his back pocket and addressed Viola.

"Can I have your name, ma'am?"

"Mrs. Viola Smith," she responded haughtily.

"Notorious gossip," Miss Fanny quipped under her breath.

Mr. Lucas turned to the woman who Viola pointed out. "And you're Autumn Randall?"

"*Mrs.* Autumn Randall," she corrected.

"Our pastor's *wife,*" Bea added.

He turned back to Viola. "And you say you have proof that Mrs. Randall committed murder?"

"I do," Viola stated with confidence, "*and* I've been told that you're only a volunteer, Mr. Lucas, so I demand that you let me speak to one of the *real* deputies."

A muscle contracted in the deputy's jaw at the less than veiled insult. "Officer Renton is out investigating the murder," he told her coolly. "The other officer is busy in the library."

His words didn't dissuade Viola. "Then I'll see him when he comes out." She turned and headed down the hallway with Lucretia and a few others on her heels.

"Aren't you going to stop her?" Bea asked Mr. Lucas. She was incensed as she hollered after her. "Now you wait a minute, Viola! I'm not going to let you poison this case with lies!" She stepped toward the door in an attempt to exit, but was blocked by Mr. Lucas.

"I suggest you simmer down, ma' am. If your friend has evidence against this woman," he indicated Autumn, "it's her duty to tell what she knows."

"Viola is *not* my friend. She's wrong! Autumn didn't kill that bus driver."

"What makes you so sure?" He asked dryly.

Bea gave an exasperated groan. "Because, I told you, I know who did it."

"You mean *we* know who did it," Miss Fanny corrected testily.

Bea threw her a look, "Okay, *we* know. The point is I've got to talk to someone in authority right now! Come on ladies."

Once again, Bea moved to step around Lucas. Once again, he blocked her. Quickly, she tried to maneuver around from the opposite direction. He was quicker.

"Mr. Lucas, would you *please* get out of the way," Connie pleaded.

"You're obstructing justice," Hattie added, pleased that she finally had a situation in which she could use the phrase.

Mr. Lucas wasn't swayed. "You're the ones obstructing justice if you withhold information." He returned his attention to Bea. "If you think you know who did it instead of the other lady, you tell *me*."

"You didn't make Viola tell you," Bea sniffed, "and she *insulted* you! So, why should I tell you anything?"

His narrowed eyes made it clear that her observation didn't please him. Turning abruptly to the cluster of women in the hall, he shouted tersely. "Ladies, nothing has changed. Your instructions were to go to your rooms. I want everybody to clear the halls and shut your doors, *now!*"

His scrawny physique and high-pitched directive didn't exude authority. Compliance was slow. When the hall was finally clear, he addressed Autumn. "I need you to go with me to the front until this is sorted out."

Autumn was huffy. "Why?"

"Because I said so," he growled gruffly.

Bea wasn't intimidated "And I take it that we can go with her since all of us in here have evidence to present, just like Viola."

She stared at Mr. Lucas hard, silently challenging him. The seconds ticked by as their eyes locked. Without wavering eye contact with her, he finally stepped aside.

"Go ahead."

Autumn led the way, with Bea, Hattie and Connie right behind her. When Miss Fanny tried to follow them, Mr. Lucas stopped her. She stood in front of him with one hand on her hip and began tapping an impatient foot.

"Is there a problem?"

Mr. Lucas stroked his chin. "I'm not sure, but I noticed when the other lady said she knew who did it, I heard you say *we* know who did it. Why don't you tell me what you know? Did you or your friend see something?"

Miss Fanny raised a suspicious brow. "Why didn't you ask that when all of us were in here together?" Was he trying to corner her because she was older and he didn't think she was as sharp as the others? Or was there another reason for this inquisition? "What are you trying to do, get ahead of the other deputies and solve this case yourself?"

She watched as Mr. Lucas' aggravated demeanor gradually changed. His face softened and his dark eyes gave the impression of sincerity.

"You know, I've been the groundskeeper here for nearly fifteen years, but being a volunteer deputy gives me more self-respect. I'm real proud of the service I provide in this community."

He paused to see what effect his declaration was having on Miss Fanny. She looked curious.

"Why are you telling me this, Mr. Lucas?"

"Because you're right. If I can break this case, it would be a real feather in my cap." He tried to evaluate her reaction to his words. She remained stoic. He pushed. "Won't you help me? Do you ladies *really* know who killed the driver?"

Miss Fanny studied him for a moment. He looked earnest, but— "Mr. Lucas..."

"Yes?" He answered eagerly.

"We're going to tell our story to Officer Renton or Officer Sims. But, good luck on your career. Now, if you'll please move, I'd like to join the others."

Like a chameleon, Lucas' manner changed so abruptly it caught Miss Fanny off guard. The look he gave her was scathing. "Thanks for nothing." He moved aside, following her to the foyer.

By the time Bea and her friends reached Viola, the hellion was engaged in a heated argument with Officer Simms. Lucretia provided backup.

"Ladies, you are interrupting my interrogation," he was telling them. "I don't have time for this nonsense. Now go to your rooms!"

"Nonsense?" Viola spat. "Young man, I hope you don't think that badge of yours gives you the right to talk to me like I was a three-year-old. I've got valuable information that can close this case."

"Don't listen to her Officer," Bea shouted as she hurried toward them.

The two campers sat on the bench enjoying the altercation. Their eyes followed the warring factions as though watching a tennis match.

Connie pointed to Viola. "Whatever she said is a lie."

"You two can't cover up for her." Lucretia shot Autumn a distrustful look. "If Viola says she has proof she has it."

"I suppose you've seen this proof?" Bea scoffed.

Lucretia hesitated. "No. But..."

"Don't you worry, *Miss Private Investigator*," Viola sneered. "I don't need a license to see what's plain as the nose on your face."

"And, just what is that?" Bea wanted to know.

"You'll see! I'll show *my* proof to a *real* investigator!"

"You're right, lady," Uncle Bud chimed in from the sidelines, enjoying the mêlée. "They already got one bootleg deputy. We don't need another one."

"Shut up!" Mr. Lucas barked entering the foyer.

The campers laughed. The women crowding the entranceway vehemently objected to their comments. The men laughed louder. Simms and Mr. Lucas shouted at both groups as they tried to keep the peace. This was the pandemonium that greeted Officer Renton when he came through the front door.

"What in the Sam Hill is going on?" He bellowed. "You were arguing when I left and you're still at it!"

Everyone in the foyer tried to speak at once. Renton roared.

"Just shut up! Simms, do you want to tell me what is going on?"

Embarrassed by his lack of control of the situation, the young officer looked tense. "I was questioning Jerry

Coolpix, when I heard this banging at the door. I came out and this one," he pointed to Viola, "started yelling at me."

Bea was quick to jump in, "I believe I can clear everything up, Officer Renton."

The weary officer turned a withering gaze her way. "I'll get to *you* in just a moment. Willie, where were you when all of this was happening?"

"I was trying to get to the bottom of this case." He indicated Miss Fanny. "This lady here claims she knows who killed the bus driver."

Simms spoke up, "And this Mrs. Smith, she says she's got *proof* of who did it."

Miss Fanny protested. "She's a fool, Officer Renton. The five of *us* really know who did it." She indicated everyone who had been in her room when she made the revelation.

The beleaguered Renton opened the door to the library and pointed at the Coolpix sitting inside. *"You, out here!"* The young man scurried into the foyer. *"You!"* Renton gestured to the six women who claimed to know the murderer. "In here!"

The women filed into the room. Closing the door behind them, he faced the group. "All of you, line up against the wall."

The women did as told. Intimidated, the ladies watched him intensely. No one spoke until Connie asked meekly, "Are you going to shoot us?"

"Don't tempt me."

Viola seized the moment. "Like I told Officer Simms, I really do know who killed the driver!"

"And just who might that be?" Renton demanded.

"Autumn Randall, that's who!" She pointed at the preacher's wife.

"That's a lie and you know it!" Autumn was livid.

"I have proof." With that, Viola reached in her pocket and triumphantly withdrew a piece of paper.

"What is that?" Bea wanted to know, taking it out of her hand.

The Officer snatched it from her grasp. "If you don't mind." He opened the paper. A cigarette butt fell to the floor. He ignored it.

Autumn gave Viola a piercing look. "Where did you get that?"

Viola raised her chin defiantly. "I found it in our room."

"You mean you invaded my privacy and *found* it in my pocket." Autumn looked as though she was about to pummel Viola.

"Invading a person's privacy is against the law!" Connie interjected. "Anyway, a piece of paper doesn't make her a murderer."

"Viola, you're a bigger fool than I thought you were," said Miss Fanny.

"I don't think that's possible," Bea interjected.

Hattie agreed. "Amen."

"Ladies, this quibbling is a waste of my time," Renton snapped. "Now tell me what this is all about." He waved the paper in the air. "And it better be good. I need to get back to investigating this case. What do you have to say, Mrs...?"

"Smith," Viola offered. "Well you might not know this, Officer, but Autumn Randall was the last one in the kitchen where the knives were kept the first day we got here. She was the only one of us outside the building that evening. She slipped in and out through the back door. I think that was when Autumn Randall went to meet her lover…"

"What?" The cry of disbelief was in unison from the ladies as well as the Officer, but it didn't stop Viola.

"It's my belief that she must have met him on the bus in the woods."

"Him, who?" Autumn looked at the others in amused astonishment as Viola continued to spin her tale.

"The bus driver," Viola addressed Renton. "They must have quarreled and she stabbed him."

The only sound in the room was the ticking of the clock on the wall, as the women stared at Viola openmouthed, amazed by her ingenuity. Renton looked equally as stunned.

"Undamnbelievable! Lady, where do you get that from? All this note says is *George, call my cell,* and it gives the number. There's no signature on it; there's nothing to indicate who wrote the note."

"How do you know that's from Autumn?" Bea demanded.

Viola continued to ignore everyone else in the room except the officer. "The area code is 317, and she told us she went for a walk, in the dark no less a*nd,* she had a flashlight. How convenient. That made it easy to find whatever she needed to find in the woods."

"Why wouldn't she have a flashlight in the woods?" Miss Fanny sneered. Viola's insanity had reached new heights.

"I wish I'd thought of bringing one with me," Hattie added.

Renton was ready to end this ridiculous spectacle. "Now, let me ask you something, Mrs. Smith. If George

Hadley was supposed to call her, why would *she* be the one with the note?"

"Anyway, that's not my number." Autumn paused dramatically, ready to let her final point strike home. "Plus, I don't have a phone with me. None of us do. Remember? We left our cell phones at home."

Viola was stumped. Smelling blood, Autumn went for the kill. Bending to pick up the cigarette butt that lay at his feet, Autumn addressed the officer.

"*This* is why I went outside, Officer Renton." She thrust the butt toward him. "I didn't want the members of my husband's church seeing me smoke. It doesn't look good. Besides, I've got enough against me on this trip and in the church community in general. I started to throw the butt away, but decided against it since I didn't want it found. After putting it out, I saw that piece of paper on the ground, picked it up and wrapped the butt in it with the intention of throwing it away later. I stuffed it in my pocket and forgot." She shrugged. "That's the whole story."

All eyes turned to Viola. This time she had a reason to avoid the condescending looks on their faces, including Offer Renton's. Looking contrite, she started to speak. The frown on his face stopped her.

"I've heard enough," he said curtly. "There's an easy way to solve this."

Officer Renton dialed the telephone number, waiting patiently until the call was answered. He got voice mail. The ladies could hear the message on the other end.

"*You know who it is. Talk to me.*"

Looking puzzled, Renton disconnected, called the number again and listened intently.

"*You know who it is. Talk to me.*"

The voice was right. Renton did know who it was.

CHAPTER 19

"I take it that it wasn't my voice you heard," Autumn stated with certainty.

"No, it wasn't." Officer Renton offered no further explanation.

"Thank you for wasting our time, Viola!" Miss Fanny chided with a roll of her eyes.

Viola was defensive. "Well, she shouldn't have been…"

"You mean, *you* shouldn't have accused someone of murder, *falsely,*" chided Connie, enjoying Viola's discomfort.

"That's called slander!" Autumn reminded her. "And I told you once that I might sue you. Now, I've got even more reason to see you in court and I've got witnesses to back me up!"

The seasoned gossip was visibly shaken. She turned pleading eyes to the officer, "All the evidence points to…"

"What evidence?" Bea challenged. "A piece of trash that Autumn found on the ground?"

"What was it doing there with the driver's first name on it?" Viola addressed Officer Renton, hoping he would validate her point. He gazed at her stone-faced.

"Mrs. Smith, is it?"

Viola nodded. "Yes, your honor."

"I'm not a judge, Mrs. Smith. But you've made whatever point you were trying to make, and it's been proven wrong. The best thing you can do now is go back to your room." He glowered menacingly. "Right *now!*"

Viola nearly tripped over her feet rushing out of the library. Renton turned his attention to the remaining would be sleuths.

"Now what's *your* story?"

Bea spoke up. "Those men out there are your murderers. They're not campers. They're drug dealers!"

She gave a dramatic pause to gauge Renton's reaction, but he didn't appear to be shocked or surprised. She could fix that.

"Not only were they *not* camping in the woods, they were here looking for places to plant marijuana! That is until they got caught in the storm." Looking smug, she finished with a flourish.

Renton asked evenly, "How do you know all this?"

Miss Fanny spoke up. "I told her, and that's just the tip of the iceberg. Those buzzards have a farm somewhere around here and they grow marijuana in their cornfields."

Renton raised a brow. "*Again*, the question is how do *you* know all this?"

"Miss Fanny and I heard it all through the vent that connects our bedroom to the front office," Autumn told him, glad that the heat was off of her. "Two of those guys were talking to each other while sitting in there waiting to be questioned."

"They didn't even know how to put up a tent," Miss Fanny relayed. "They said it blew away. What kind of mess is that?"

Leaving the lineup, Bea walked up to Renton—facing him, detective to detective. "You see, Officer Renton, logic tells me that when the storm started, the Coolpixs' were wandering around trying to find their car when they came across the bus and the bus driver. Maybe they knew him or maybe they met him by accident, but at any rate they ended up killing him."

Simultaneously, four heads bobbed up and down in agreement. None of the women could determine what the officer was thinking as he studied the assemblage. Chuckling, he shook his head in amusement.

"Ladies, I have to tell you, this has to be one of the most interesting lineups in the history of law enforcement."

"But we're not the suspects," Bea protested. "They are!" She pointed toward the door where the three men sat on the other side.

Renton didn't respond. Instead he looked from them to the closed door and back again. He stroked his chin before addressing no one in particular.

"When was the last time you ladies saw the bus driver alive?"

The women agreed that it was when he and Mr. Lucas transported their food supplies from the bus to the kitchen.

"We were having a meeting in the dining room." Bea added. "We didn't notice him leave. At least I didn't." Her cohorts confessed they hadn't noticed either.

"So, you don't remember whether he left by the back door or the front door?" Renton wanted to know. No one did.

He looked at the crumpled piece of paper in his hand and then at Autumn. "And you were in the front or the back of this place when you were smoking?"

She looked confused by the question. "I was in the back."

Autumn's eyes slid to Bea, giving her a questioning look that asked why he wanted to know that. Bea wondered too, and was about to ask when Renton walked to the library door, flung it open and stepped into the foyer. Eager to witness the campers' downfall, the five women crowded in the doorway. Bea, Hattie and Connie nudged each other proudly, glad to have helped solve another crime.

The foyer was quiet. The Coolpixs were still sitting on the bench. Officer Simms was lounging in a chair, while Mr. Lucas slouched against a wall by the front door looking bored. Both officers snapped to attention when Renton appeared.

"Is everything okay?" asked Simms.

Renton nodded. His eyes moved from Simms to Lucas and then to each of the campers. He gazed at them for so long that they began to squirm.

"What?" Uncle Bud asked. "Don't tell me those old biddies have been in there telling more lies!"

Officer Renton remained silent. He took his cell phone out, read the number on the paper that Viola had given him and called the number again. His eyes roamed the room as he waited for voice mail. When it answered, he left a cryptic message.

"It's Officer Renton. I've got you." He disconnected.

"What's he doing?" Connie whispered to Bea.

"Setting a trap for those three smart alecks," she whispered back. "Of course I'm only speculating." But she was pretty sure she was right.

"Gentlemen, I'd like to ask if I could see each of your cell phones." Officer Renton asked the Coolpixs politely.

"For what?" Jerry looked at him suspiciously.

"There should be no objection to my simply looking at them," Renton answered smoothly. "Of course none of you are under arrest so you don't have to comply."

"Oh, he's good," Hattie told Connie. "He's like the cops on TV."

"But a little less confrontational," Bea observed, making note of his method so she could use it in future cases. Maybe Officer Renton was smarter than she thought.

The Coolpix brothers looked to Uncle Bud for guidance. He removed his cell from his pants pocket and so did Jerry.

"Mine is over there." Walter got up and headed for the coat rack where his jacket was hanging. Officer Renton stopped him.

"I'll do the honors." Walking toward the rack, he tossed a directive to Lucas. "Go back there and check on those women, Willie. Make sure they're still in their rooms. We don't need any more confusion around here. Oh, and write the room numbers down for me too, will you? I might need them."

Mr. Lucas disappeared down the hallway. Officer Renton took down one of the two jackets hanging on the rack.

"Mine's the green one, not the blue one," Walter quickly informed him.

Renton didn't acknowledge him. Removing the cell phone he found in the pocket he pushed a button before putting the phone back.

"What's he doing?" Autumn asked no one in particular. Since nobody knew, nobody answered.

Renton then went to the green jacket and handed it to the young man.

"Thank all three of you for your cooperation. Now, I want each of you to show me a list of your recent calls."

"Why is he being so nice to those scoundrels?" Miss Fanny complained. "He needs to bring the hammer down on them."

"He will," Bea assured her, admiring his smooth operation. "Just watch."

The campers looked wary. Uncle Bud spoke up.

"I don't think we need to do all that. You said you just wanted to look at our phones. Like you said, we're not under arrest so we don't have to do none of this if we don't want to."

The officer shrugged. "Okay."

Mr. Lucas reappeared in the foyer. "All the women are in their rooms. They're not happy about it though." He handed Renton the list of room numbers.

Renton glanced at it briefly, then asked, "Call the office and tell them we're going to need some more help out here."

Withdrawing his cell phone, Lucas did as told. Renton turned to the women in the doorway.

"Go to your rooms, ladies! I've got business to conduct here."

Not daring to object, they left the library slowly shuffled toward the hallway. Bea had a question in passing.

"Are you sure you don't want us out here with you when...?" She shot a glance at the campers. "Uh, you know?"

Ignoring her, Officer Renton directed his attention to Simms. "See that these ladies get in the back and make sure they stay there."

Bea was insulted. "Well, I never!" The warm feelings she'd had earlier toward him faded—again—especially when he entered the deserted library and shut the door in her face.

While Lucas was making his phone call, Officer Simms turned his attention to the gathering.

"All right, ladies, let's move." His order was met with scornful glares.

As the quintet moved slowly down the hall, in the foyer the muffled sound of a ringing telephone could be heard. *Ring! Ring! Ring!*

Miss Fanny peeked back and hollered at the men. "Can't y'all hear that phone?" She motioned toward the coat rack. "It sounds like it's coming from that blue jacket right there." The phone kept ringing.

Distracted, Officer Simms called to the jacket's owner. "Willie, why don't you answer the call?"

The door to the library opened. Officer Renton appeared in the doorway. In one hand he held his cell phone. In his other hand he held the scrap of paper given to him by Viola Smith. He looked at his volunteer deputy.

"Yes, Willie, now that I've turned the ringer on, why *don't* you answer it?"

****

"What's happening?" Hattie whispered to Bea as the women hovered against the wall in the hallway trying to look inconspicuous. "Why is Officer Renton mad at Mr. Lucas over a cell phone?"

"Shhh, I'm trying to listen," Bea warned, straining to hear the conversation between the deputy and his superior officer. A somber looking Mr. Lucas was trying to explain the second phone in his coat. He sounded defensive.

"I forgot about that phone. It's just a throwaway I bought a while ago. I don't use it often."

The Officer nodded, but didn't look convinced. "And what about *this*?" He waved the paper in his hand. "It has that cell phone number on it."

Bea started. The connection between the ringing phone in the jacket and the paper with the telephone number began to dawn on her. The implication became apparent to her cohorts as well.

"Ooooweeee," Miss Fanny shrieked loud enough to attract Simms' attention. He charged toward them.

"Ladies, didn't I tell you to..."

Miss Fanny sailed past him addressing the senior officer. "So, it was him who wrote that number and not them drug dealers?"

"Drug dealers!" Uncle Buddy leaped to his feet.

Miss Fanny told him what she and Autumn heard, leaving out the vent as their source. The uproar was immediate.

"You're lying through your false teeth!" Uncle Bud declared.

"We don't know nothing about no marijuana!" Jerry hollered.

"Who said anything about marijuana?" Miss Fanny countered.

"You're just trying to pin that murder on us!" Walter started toward Miss Fanny who looked determined to do some serious damage if the man came any closer. Officer Renton stopped him with a jerk of his arm, and directed Miss Fanny out of the foyer with a firm nod. She complied and he returned his attention to the men.

"If you guys didn't have anything to do with this

murder, then why did I find three pairs of muddy footprints on the steps of the bus?" Renton asked him. *"And* near the body?"

He glanced down at the mud caked on the men's shoes.

"That means they were on the bus after it started raining," Bea whispered to the others.

"But we found the body *before* then," Hattie observed.

"Which means they might not have done it," Connie concluded, sounding disappointed.

"Well, I'm glad the heats off of me," Autumn said with relief.

The quartet continued to eavesdrop. Walter Coolpix was livid. "Hadley was dead when we found him! All we were trying to do was get out of the rain."

Jerry was close to hyperventilating. "We didn't even know that man was George Hadley until we got here and heard it from you guys."

"Oh *really*?' Renton raised a brow.

"Jerry!" Uncle Bud warned, whirling on his nephew.

The young man looked frantic. "I'm not goin' down on no murder charge. Hell, weed is small potatoes compared to that."

"Shut up!" Walter grabbed at his brother. Renton kept them apart. Simms moved in to help him, while Lucas stayed huddled near the front door trying to look as inconspicuous as the ladies.

"The rats are about to turn on each other." Bea observed the entire scenario with a satisfied grin.

"What do you have to say to me, Jerry?" Renton prompted.

"Don't you say a word," Uncle Bud threatened.

Renton raised the stakes. "Talk or I'll take you in for suspicion of murder."

Jerry's eyes widened. "I'm telling you, we didn't do it. I'm not going to jail for murder! All we been doing is growing weed for the guy who runs the dope business in these parts…"

"I'm gonna kick your ass, Jerry!" Walter lunged for him. Simms held him back.

"You mother…," Uncle Buddy drew back a fist to hit his nephew. Renton quickly restrained him. Jerry kept talking.

"The headman's a major player, runs this whole area. But, we've never seen him and don't know his name."

Looking alarmed, Uncle Bud dropped down on the bench heavily. "Man, be quiet, or we're gonna end up like Hadley for sure."

Renton jumped on his mistake instantly. "So you *did* know Hadley.

Uncle Bud gave him a look that told the officer where to go. Walter dropped down beside him, folded his arms across his chest and looked straight ahead, but the threat of death didn't stop Jerry.

"We never even heard of this Hadley guy before. A few days ago he called from Indianapolis and said he found out about us from the head honcho down here. He said he would be in this area and wanted to talk to us about working for *him*. We were supposed to meet Hadley about starting a meth…"

"Jerry! I swear to God, I'll kill you if you say another word," Uncle Bud spat. This time his nephew looked intimidated, but Renton kept hammering.

"From what you're saying it sounds like Hadley was cutting the mysterious Mr. X out of the deal with you guys and was trying to start a new business."

"We don't have nothin' to say without a lawyer," Uncle Bud told him. "Either arrest us or let us go."

Officer Renton shrugged. "That's your constitutional right." He paused and glanced over at the surly looking Lucas before refocusing on the men. "I want the three of you in the library. This area needs to be cleared."

Cutting their eyes at the traitorous Jerry, the campers complied. Renton turned to Simms and started to speak when he became aware of the ladies huddling in the hall. His voice rose in frustration as he stormed toward them.

"How many times do I have to tell you women to go to your rooms!"

"Don't you need some testimony from us?" Bea wanted to know.

"We can be of help," Connie told him. She lowered her voice so that only he could hear what she had to say. "After all, we're the only ones who saw Mr. Lucas and Mr. Hadley together and..."

Officer Renton called to Simms. "Take these ladies back there, and make sure that there are no women in that first bedroom to your left. When you get back up here, I'll be in the office talking to Willie. I want you to guard the library door and make certain that our guests stay put."

As instructed, Simms checked the first bedroom. found it empty and then escorted his charges back to Bea's room, near the dining hall. After closing the door behind them, he returned to the foyer.

Bea, Hattie and Connie didn't wait long until they sprang into action. After formulating a plan, Hattie peeked out the door to make sure all was clear.

"All set," she informed the others.

"You going with us?" Bea asked Autumn and Miss Fanny. Both ladies declined.

"I'm not going to jail with you fools," Miss Fanny declared.

In bare feet, the ace detectives stole into the hallway, hugging the wall. Cautiously, listening for every sound, they inched their way toward their intended goal——the forbidden bedroom. Reaching their destination without being detected, they entered and shut the door quietly behind them and then hunkered down in front of the vent.

"You can deny it all you want, Willie," Renton was saying, "but I compared the numbers you wrote in the notebook with the numbers on this piece of paper and the writing is the same. Plus, my voice is on the cell phone in *your* coat, and this is the telephone number I called. It was found behind the center, where you and Hadley stopped to talk after going out the back door. I suspect he thought he put it in his pocket, but it dropped to the ground."

For a moment there was silence. Lucas made no comment. Renton continued.

"This is how I see it. *You're* the drug kingpin around here. I'll give you credit, you've stayed under the radar. Nobody knew what you looked like, and I've got to confess, if it wasn't for this phone and this number I never would have suspected you."

Renton paused. Again, Lucas didn't respond.

"I think that, unintentionally, you dropped the names of those three underlings of yours during a conversation with Hadley. More likely than not, on that extra cell phone that you use for drug deals. Now, it's my guess that Hadley was trying to do a side deal with the Coolpixs. You found out about it and killed him."

With that accusation, Lucas finally spoke. "And how did I do that?" he asked sarcastically.

"I don't know, maybe you drove ahead of his bus, stopped your car and flagged him down telling him you had car trouble. Or maybe you followed his bus. However you got him to stop, he did it because he had no reason not to trust you. He had no idea who you really were, but you knew him. And when he turned his back, that's when you stabbed him with the knife you stole out of the center's kitchen."

Mr. Lucas sounded incredulous. "I am a *volunteer* deputy! How could you think I would do the things you're accusing me of?"

"It's easy. If I was a criminal, I can't think of a better place to be than right in the middle of law enforcement activity where I could keep up with what's going on. I've got to admit that you're clever."

"Who me?" Mr. Lucas's tone was laced with contempt. "I'm just a groundskeeper, nothing more, nothing less."

"You're wrong. Right now, you're a suspect in the murder of Mr. George Hadley."

While Officer Renton read a protesting Mr. Lucas his rights, Bea, Hattie and Connie gave each other high fives, silently congratulating themselves for helping solve another crime. Even if they had guessed the wrong culprit, initially, no matter, justice was served. That's what Grandmothers, Incorporated was about!

They were about to steal out of the room and back down the hall when they were stopped in their tracks by additional words coming from the vent. It was a command from Officer Renton.

"Ladies, you can stop listening now and I want to see whoever is in that bedroom up front."

CHAPTER 20

They were busted! For a moment the three women stood frozen in place.

"How did he know we were listening?" Connie wanted to know.

"I'm not sure," answered Bea, and with grudging admiration added, "but he's *good*."

"We better go face the music," Hattie said glumly.

Looking like condemned prisoners marching to the gallows, the three women entered the foyer. Willie Lucas was sitting in a chair, while the campers were back on the bench. All four men were hand-cuffed. Officer Simms stood guard. A stern looking Officer Renton stood in the office door.

The ladies couldn't help but stare at Mr. Lucas. He didn't fit the image of a drug kingpin. If they hadn't overheard the interrogation with their own ears, they never would have believed it.

As she passed him, Bea couldn't resist aiming a parting shot at Lucas. "Justice prevails."

"Ladies!" Renton barked sharply, jabbing a finger toward the room. "In here!" Once they were all inside, he slammed the door.

"He sure does a lot of door slamming," Connie muttered under her breath. "He should work on that temper."

The women took seats across from the desk where Renton perched. He stared long and hard at the group sitting in front of him.

"I heard you talking about justice out there." He looked pointedly at Bea. "I have to say that you ladies deserve a bit of that yourselves."

Bea perked up, "You don't have to thank us, Officer Renton. As a licensed detective, I'm always willing..."

"Can you *ever* be quiet?" He shot her a lethal look. Bea thought it best to make silence a virtue at the moment.

Barely containing his anger, Renton began pacing. "I figured I could count on you three to disregard my instructions not to go back in that room and I thank you for not letting me down."

"How did you know we were in there?" Hattie asked sheepishly, hoping they hadn't broken any laws. She wouldn't do well in jail.

"The sounds from that vent go both ways. After interrogating Willie, I heard some rustling coming from that room."

Connie lifted a brow. "Rustling?"

"Yes, *rustling.* You ladies need to learn to move more quietly."

Bea remained silent, but filed that information away for future reference.

"All I've got to say is that you three are a piece of work."

"Thank you," Hattie offered graciously. She was unsure of his meaning, but what he had to say sounded good.

"No, thank *you.*" Renton's voice dripped with sarcasm. "I want to thank you for interfering with a police investigation, tampering with evidence, and contaminating a crime scene." He turned to Connie. "And let's not forget assault with a deadly weapon."

His last comment drew vehement protests.

"Are you telling me I couldn't stop an intruder from breaking in and killing every one of us?" Connie fumed.

"Besides, you ought to be fussing at that meddling Viola Smith for snooping through people's personal belongings!" Hattie fumed.

Bea broke her silence. She wouldn't stand for him questioning her integrity.

"*Officer* Renton, I'll have you know that I took great pains to preserve the crime scene. We touched nothing."

"Except you touched the blood," Hattie added helpfully.

Shooting her a look, Bea hurried on. "Furthermore, pointing you to the real criminal took true detective work, and I, sir, am a *true* detective." Reaching into her pocket, she retrieved a wallet sized copy of her detective license. She pushed it toward him.

Ignoring her and her license, the beleaguered officer held up both hands and let out a heavy sigh. "I'll concede that if that conversation between the Coolpixs hadn't been overheard, I would have had to do some additional police work to get to the bottom of this case."

"Aha!" Bea shrilled.

"And what about the telephone number on that piece of paper?" Connie reminded him.

"It sounds like you wouldn't even have a case if it hadn't been for the women in this center," said an emboldened Hattie.

A besieged Renton looked ready to scream. Instead, he offered the annoying trio an olive branch.

"Taking that into consideration, I'm going to forget all the charges that I should bring against you, if you promise to *quickly* pack your things and go home."

"We will!" Three heads shook eagerly in agreement.

"And please, don't come back here again—at least not to my jurisdiction."

Three voices spoke in unison. "We won't!"

The exhausted officer leaned against the wall. "It's been a long night and tomorrow will probably be longer. I'll contact the bus company that provided your transportation and tell them to send another one to take you home..."

"On Sunday," Hattie finished his sentence. "We paid to be here until then."

He looked at her steadily. "Inform all of the women with you that they should get packed. You'll be going home as *soon* as the bus arrives." There were no further objections.

As the ladies left the office, they were greeted by flashing red lights shining through the windows. Officers had arrived to take Lucas and the Coolpix family to jail.

"Mrs. Bell, please tell Mrs. Collier and Mrs. Randall that I'll be contacting them. All of you might be needed to give further statements."

"I certainly will."

"And Mrs. Palmer. I will be returning your gun." Connie thanked him with a wide smile.

Hours later, the ladies stood at the front door as Officers Simms and Renton left for their cruiser with their prisoners in tow. Looking back, Officer Renton tipped his hat to them got into his squad car and drove off.

Bea emitted a satisfied sigh. "Well ladies, it looks like Grandmothers, Incorporated has done it again."

****

The sun was shining brightly on the rain-washed forest and its warm rays were streaming through the windows of the center's dining room. Breakfast had been served. The dishes were cleared, washed and put away. Everyone was gathered in the room and sat in rapt attention ready for the day's announcements. The ladies were excited about going home. Thelma and Dorothy stood in front of them.

"Attention ladies," Dorothy called the group to order. "Officer Simms came by earlier this morning to tell us that the bus should be here by noon!"

After the cheering died down, Dorothy continued. "And I'm glad to announce that we will be driven back to Indianapolis by the Road Wanderers regular driver, Mr. Sweeney." This time the cheering was accompanied by thunderous applause. "We've asked everyone to check their rooms to make sure nothing has been left." Looking serious, Dorothy pulled her glasses down on her nose and peered over them. "If anyone here forgets something, that's on you, so don't ask us to come back and get it. Thelma, do you have your report?"

Thelma nodded. "The grounds have been checked for debris, the meeting rooms and dining area are spotless. The trash has been bagged and put outside in the proper bins. As for the kitchen, it's been thoroughly checked. All of the pots, pans, dishes and silverware have been accounted for, and the borrowed knives have been put back in place." She paused. "Except for one."

"And we know where that one is," Miss Fanny called out.

Hattie rolled her eyes at her mother-in-law. Leave it to her to bring that up. A temporary pall fell over the gathering at the memory of the slain driver. Dorothy quickly spoke up.

"But, thank God, all of that is behind us. Now, before we leave Hattie Collier is going to say a few words."

That bit of news brought a few groans, but most of the attendees were accommodating. Hattie cleared her throat as she stood before the group.

"I'd like to thank Thelma and Dorothy for doing a wonderful job organizing our trip. I think it went quite well..."

"Other than the murder," someone added.

"And almost being attacked by those campers..."

"Don't forget, being questioned by the police..."

"And some of you nearly being arrested."

Enduring the comments, Hattie forged on. Dead bus driver or not, she had an agenda to get through.

"We all know the purpose of our retreat was to commune with nature, get close to God, and to become closer to each other as Christian women."

Angela Rivers chuckled loudly "Nothing will get you closer to God than fearing for your life!"

Several of the women snickered at her comment. Hattie kept going.

"The point *is* that in spite of all that's happened, we accomplished some of what we came here to do."

"Yes we did," Gladys Hodges piped in, "especially the getting closer to nature part."

"Thank you, Gladys." Hattie was pleased that someone was contributing positively. "Would you like to share with the group how this trip made that happen for you? What did you learn?"

"I learned that when you pee in the woods, bring some toilet paper. Don't use leaves. You could get poison ivy."

For a second, the comment Gladys made left everyone speechless, before the laughter began. Ruth Rivers spoke up.

"I learned that you can get plenty of exercise on a retreat, especially when you're running for your life through the woods. I didn't know these old legs could move that fast."

Her daughter, Angela, was laughing so hard she could hardly breathe. "Mom...momma left me in a cloud of dust," she managed to say. "All I could see was arms and legs."

The entire gathering was laughing hysterically as they vied to recall their hasty retreat to safety and their frantic efforts to keep the campers out of the center.

Hattie began laughing too. "The Lord *does* work in mysterious ways. When we were all afraid for our lives, we managed to put many of our differences aside for a while and find ways to protect ourselves and each other."

Her words caused some somber reflection as a hush descended over the group. Autumn Randall stood up.

"Ladies, Hattie has a point. There were times during these last few days when we showed that we really could band together when we had to. I see that as progress, no matter how small. I'd like that spark of solidarity to grow."

Her comments were met by applause. After the clapping ceased, Viola rose to her feet. Slowly, tentatively, she walked up to Autumn. Instantly, the mood in the room shifted to one of anxious anticipation. Instinctively, Autumn braced herself for a verbal assault.

Squaring her shoulders, Viola looked the young first lady in her eyes and spoke loud enough for everyone present to hear.

"I've been thinking about how I've treated you, and it wasn't very Christian like."

"Amen to that," Miss Fanny grunted.

Viola continued. "Sometimes we don't do the right thing and we've got to fix that, and that's what I want to do." She took a shaky breath. "I'm sorry I gave you such a hard time. I was wrong."

Everyone was thunderstruck, but no one more than Autumn. For a moment she was speechless. The room was quiet enough to hear a pin drop. Autumn finally found her voice.

"Thank you, Viola, I really appreciate that." She started to offer her a hug, changed it to a handshake and to her surprise—and everyone else's—Viola took the younger woman into her embrace.

"Hallelujah!" Hattie rejoiced.

Impressed, Miss Fanny decided to give credit where credit was due. "That took courage for you to approach Autumn and say that to her, Viola. It's appreciated by us all." The ladies agreed with a round of applause.

Hattie grinned. She winked at Dorothy and Thelma. "Maybe this conference wasn't such a bad idea after all."

EPILOGUE

At noon, the women gathered in front of the center to welcome the bus. Mr. Sweeney, short, round faced and with a smile as big as Texas, stepped off to bask in the warm welcome he received. Dorothy, Thelma and the three Grandmothers, Incorporated sleuths were the last to board.

"What happened, Mr. Sweeney? Thelma wanted to know. "Why didn't you drive us here? Were you ill?"

Mr. Sweeney scratched his head. "It was the weirdest thing, the morning before the trip me and George had breakfast together at this greasy spoon. The next thing you know, I was sick as a dog. The doctor said it was food poisoning. Luckily enough, George was available for an emergency run. He had been bugging me about taking you guys down here. Poor guy, all he wanted to do was earn a few extra bucks."

Giving each other knowing looks, the ladies remained silent.

The trip home was as different as night and day. Occasionally, the sound of laughter floated through the bus, but the arguing and sniping had ceased. Looking pleased, Hattie softly hummed "Onward Christian Soldiers".

Bea and Connie sat together recounting their latest adventure. Bea couldn't wait to get home to tell her son, Bryant, how they helped solve another case.

She gushed, "Despite some setbacks, this had been one exciting trip."

"Viola thinks so," said Connie. "Just because she found some lousy piece of paper—by snooping—she and her sidekick, Lucretia, think they can be detectives now.

They asked me did I think they could join Grandmothers, Incorporated."

"What!" Bea nearly choked on the snack she was eating. "Are you kidding me?"

Connie laughed. "I wish I was."

Bea growled. "I hope you told her a big fat *hell no!*" They both cringed at the thought of those two incompetents fighting against crime.

"Hey, ladies!" Mr. Sweeney's voice boomed over the bus intercom. "How about a movie? I brought something I thought you would like. Thelma, will you do the honors."

It turned out to be the Denzel Washington movie they had tried to watch on their way to the retreat. The ladies groaned, but the music faded and the actor began to speak. A loud cheer rose from the group.

"It's in *English*!" someone happily exclaimed.

Mr. Sweeney looked perplexed. "You all sure are excited over a movie. What happened at that conference? Was it that boring?"

A chorus of woman shouted back at him. "What happened at the conference *stays* at the conference!"

THE END

ABOUT THE AUTHORS

L. Barnett Evans is a novelist, playwright, and award-winning storyteller. She has given spoken-word performances at schools, churches, art festivals and various other venues across the country. She has written several plays: *Is God Calling My Name?, North Star,* and *The Body of Christ.* She has also written for newspapers and magazines. Her novel, *And All the People Said...*is a suspense thriller. Her comedy fiction, *Grandmothers, Incorporated* was her first collaborative effort and was co-written with C. V. Rhodes. Barnett Evans also collaborated with Rhodes on the play, *Grandmothers, Incorporated* which enjoyed a successful Off-Broadway run. Barnett Evans holds a Bachelor degree in Business Administration. Visit her website at: www.lilliebarnettevans.com

C. V. Rhodes is an author and an award-winning playwright and author. Her comedy fiction, novel, *Grandmothers, Incorporated,* co-written with L. Barnett Evans, was selected as Best Book of the Year by two online websites. Her romance suspense novels and women's fiction novels include: *Sin, Sweet Sacrifice, Sinful Intentions, Singing a Song, Small Sensations, Still Water., Secrets, Stranger Shadows of Love, Someone Like Me, Someone Like You* and *Someone Like Them.* As a playwright she has been the recipient of the BTA Award for the Best Original Writing for her stage play, *Stoops.* Written Word Magazine named Rhodes as one of the Ten Up and Coming Authors in the Midwest. Rhodes holds a Masters degree in Sociology and has written for newspapers magazines, radio and television. Visit her website at www.crystalrhodes.com.

Evans and Rhodes website:
www.grandmothersinc.com

www.ingramcontent.com/pod-product-compliance
Lightning Source LLC
Chambersburg PA
CBHW070525260626
47161CB00004B/1635